Girl Cries So Pretty

An Ella Porter Mystery Thriller

Georgia Wagner

Contents

Prologue

Stillness descended like the last gasp of a dying man, the stars glimmering in the inky night sky above them. Gabe and Mary stood in awed silence, taking in the sight before them. The snow-tipped mountains dreamt in the distant horizon, and the air was clear and crisp.

Their minds had wandered to other places, and as they waited in anticipation for the Northern Lights to come, they found themselves more excited with each passing moment.

Gabe nudged his girlfriend, glancing over at the college Freshman. She returned his coy smile, and leaned against him, her head resting against his shoulder, the two of them staring at the sky.

Out here, with no light pollution, the shimmering stars spread across the horizon.

They were alone.

Very alone.

Gabe could hear the sound of Mary breathing, and it calmed his anxieties a bit. He glanced nervously off into the trees for what felt like the millionth time since they set up their small, insulated, orange tent.

"There are no bears!" Mary insisted, adding a little chuckle to show she wasn't annoyed just exasperated.

He appreciated this about her.

She always took time to tend to his feelings. He'd never dated anyone as considerate as her.

It had been her idea to come out here on their first Alaskan date.

"Wow," he whispered, "The stars... I've never seen so many."

She looked up as well and chuckled. "The lower forty-eight doesn't have stars?"

"No... I mean, Chicago does... But damn... We can't see this many. It looks like a... a..."

"A what?"

"I dunno... Something cool, though."

They both giggled at his inability to grasp a metaphor. In his mind, he thought it resembled a field of diamonds. Like the diamond he wanted to give *her* later this evening.

They'd been dating online for nearly two years now, and she'd visited him every other month down in Illinois.

This was the first time he'd been able to save the money to come north.

It was a special moment.

To propose under a horizon streaked with brilliant stars...

His anxiety at the thought of bears or wolves creeping through the woods was replaced by a rising sense of excitement.

"You know," Mary said, "I once heard there are over a hundred billion stars in a galaxy."

He glanced at her. "Are you serious?" He felt his awe return as he glanced up at the star-speckled darkness.

"Guess how many galaxies there are?"

"Dunno."

"Guess, Gabe."

"Ummm... Ten million."

She giggled. "Close. Two trillion."

He looked at her fully now, certain she was teasing. But she just looked certain now. "Do you ever wonder..." she said softly, her breath fogging on the air, "How all of this could've just... *arrived*." She tried snapping her fingers, but her gloves stopped it. "A hundred billion stars in a galaxy. Two trillion galaxies. And the known universe might only be a small sliver of the *actual* universe. It's crazy to think it all came from nothing."

Here, Gabe wrinkled his nose and hid a sigh. Sometimes, Mary would veer off into the existential and it made his head hurt. Not to mention, he had his own plans for tonight instead of a long, drawn-out, philosophical debate.

He cleared his throat, hoping the small noise might distract her.

She paused, her nose wrinkling in that cute way it often did when she was puzzling over some complex problem. The two of them were still staring at the stars...

But then, another noise, this one almost as close, shattered the silence, causing the young couple to jump in surprise. Gabe whirled around, staring towards the tall, dark green boughs reaching towards the sky.

The sound repeated itself, like a faint *thumping* of wood on snow.

"Did you hear that?" he whispered fiercely.

Mary was no longer star-gazing and instead had slipped her hand into his, holding tight. "What was that?" she whispered fiercely.

The sound came again, and it sent a chill down their spines; they held their breaths in fear.

It had to be a bear.

Gabe scrambled for his fanny pack, his fingers trembling to find the zipper.

"And you teased me for wearing this," he muttered.

"Shh, it might hear us!"

He unzipped the bag and pulled out a small, metallic canister, still fumbling to orient the device. He clicked the safety lock on the bear spray and held it up, his other hand tightly clenching Mary's.

They both stared towards the prickling Sitka spruce trees. The tall branches waved on the breeze.

A new shiver erupted down his spine.

The sound had faded now, replaced by the whine of the wind. The two of them were hours away from Juneau. The capital of Alaska.

The damn place had no roads leading into it, so Gabe had been forced to charter a small plane.

That alone had cost a fortune for him, especially after saving up for the ring.

But now, his trembling hand slipped from Mary's to zip the small bag closed again. He didn't want to risk her seeing the cube-shaped velvet box.

But then, there was another cracking sound, and Mary yelped.

"I think it's coming closer!" she whispered.

"No... No, I think we're fine. Let's just head back to the tent!"

"No—no, it's still there!" she retorted hurriedly.

The two of them remained motionless for a moment. Gabe frowned, thinking of his father—a high-powered attorney in Chicago. A man's man with a barrel chest and a beard.

If his old man ever saw him cowering next to his girl instead of *doing* something to assuage her fears, he'd never hear the end of it.

It took all his courage, but he summoned what small resolve he had and slipped his hand from hers.

"Where are you going?" she whispered fiercely.

"I'm just going to the tent," he replied back, softly. "I'll grab the lights and the noise makers. It'll scare him off."

"What about the gun?"

"W-what?"

"I brought my mom's gun."

"You did?"

"Duh. This is Alaska."

"Okay... okay... Shit. You wait here, I'll get the gun."

"No... No, what if it sees you."

He wanted to point out that they still didn't even know what *it* was.

"Probably just a squirrel," he said with a laugh he didn't feel at all. He tried to put a brave face on it, channeling Gabe Sr.

Then, with far more swagger than he felt, he trod through the packed snow, towards the tree line, using the tip of the orange tent they'd set up as a marker.

As he approached, he felt his pulse quicken.

He heard a *crunch*.

Gabe froze, his muscles tensing as he strained to listen. There was silence for a few moments before he heard the crunching sound again. This time, it was closer. His hands shook as he aimed the bear spray towards the trees.

Then another sound. Behind him.

He glanced sharply back to find Mary following in his footsteps, refusing to let him brave the bear alone.

Or was it a wolf?

Or worse?

He shivered but felt a small amount of relief that she was coming towards him.

The two of them stepped into the clearing where they'd set up their tent...

And then they saw it.

They both froze.

Both of them gaping, eyes wide, mouths unhinged.

It was as if the darkness faded, briefly. As if the stars themselves were illuminating the shape in the tree.

In the darkness, something appeared, suspended from a tree, arms outstretched like some angel of light.

A figure.

A wraith-like figure in the tree.

They screamed in panicked confusion, both stumbling back.

Gabe and Mary stared, their eyes wide with fear as they looked up, trying to make sense of the figure they were now facing.

And then realization settled its grim hooks into them.

What they saw was a corpse, hanging from a branch, a noose around its neck, the body swaying slightly in the wind.

Arms spread by barbed wire, head tilted to the side.

Gabe's hand shook as he clutched the bear spray, his eyes darting around in the darkness. There was no sign of anyone else, and the only sound was their ragged breathing.

Suddenly the Northern Lights appeared high in the sky, their colors, their shapes, their undulating waves of light. The lights were the shapes of flower petals, the colors scattering and shifting.

It was like the most beautiful, serene version of a disco ball Gabe had ever seen.

Though even this characterization felt shallow in his mind.

But the beauty and awe of the lights was lost on him.

The vibrant hues shone and flashed over the corpse in the tree like fireworks.

A colorless, lifeless face stared down at them.

And then the eyes fluttered.

The woman on the tree let out a faint groan.

"Please..." she whispered, her voice hoarse.

And Gabe yelled in surprise.

"She's alive!" Mary screamed. "Gabe, she's alive!"

The woman, who he'd taken to be a corpse—arms outstretched, wire holding her aloft—let out a long sigh, blinking under the dancing lights, and then her head fell again, her eyes fluttering shut.

Chapter 1

Ella Porter peered through the window of the small bi-plane, her foot tapping nervously. They were flying over the ocean to reach Juneau, and she still hated the ocean.

But it was either fly or arrive by boat to the capital city of Alaska. And with *this* case, her higher-ups had insisted she take the trip.

A low whistle emanated at her side. "There are really no roads leading here?"

She glanced over at Brenner Gunn, reaching up to brush her hair from her eyes, the sunlight causing it to look like spun gold. Her pale blue eyes reflected in the glass of the window on the small plane, and her upturned, celestial nose gave a hesitant little sniff as she caught a hint of Brenner's sandalwood aftershave.

"Holy shit!" he exclaimed. Shifting a bit and favoring his right side.

She tried not to stare, but every now and then, she felt a pang of guilt as she realized his recovery from being shot two months ago was a slow-going thing.

At his words, though, fear jolted through her.

"What?" she looked over, startled, her heart leaping as her mind filled with images of tumbling from the sky into the frigid, choppy waters below.

But Brenner was staring at his phone, his eyebrows high on his head.

With the way the sun caught his silhouette, she was reminded that her childhood sweetheart had gotten even prettier with age. He was over six foot, with those blue eyes and a chiseled jaw emphasized, in a way, by the single burn mark under the side of his chin and up to his left ear. He scratched at it, studying his phone with his solemn gaze which always carried a tinge of sadness.

Now, though, his eyes were widened, and he gave a low whistle.

"What is it?"

"Nothing, just..." Suddenly, he swallowed, glancing awkwardly at her. "Nothing."

She hesitated, frowning.

As if sensing her curiosity, he quickly said, "Looks like we're descending. Chat later."

The plane was beginning to drop from its high altitude, and it caused her stomach to tighten as it so often did.

"Conversation distracts me," she said firmly. It wasn't normal for Ella Porter to insist on anything. She'd often found that one caught more flies with honey.

She was somewhat famous, during her come-up at the FBI, before *the incident* that got her banished, for being extra polite and patient in the face of obnoxious witnesses or coworkers.

But with Brenner... she felt as if she could be more honest. He'd taken a bullet on behalf of her family. On behalf of her sister, in fact.

They still hadn't talked about it. Brenner didn't want to bring it up.

This was his first week back on the job, though, and she had to admit it was somewhat relieving to see him up and around.

Besides, honesty with Brenner was something he often asked of her...

Or, more accurately, *required* of her.

"What is it?" she said.

"Nothing, just... have you seen the victims?"

She stared at him. "One was married to an ex-con, right? That's why you're tagging along."

"Er, yeah. Plus, you know, slow day with the Marshals."

She frowned at him.

Then he turned the phone for her to see, and she went still. She blinked, staring at the phone, looking at the faces of their victims for the first time. At least, faces that weren't framed by the metal of an operating table in a coroner's office.

"Is it true that the third victim was alive when they found her?"

"She died not long after they found," Ella said quietly. "But not befo re..." She trailed off, staring at the pictures.

"Hot, right?" Brenner said.

She glanced at him then back at the photos.

The word *hot* didn't quite do the three women justice.

Ella had never seen such gorgeous women in her life. She didn't consider herself an *unattractive* person, though, she often wore hand-me-down clothing from second-hand stores. Most things she purchased weren't new.

She didn't have pierced ears and despised any golden jewelry. Gold reminded her too much of her family.

But compared to these three...

She felt a flutter, remembering days back in high school, where inse-curity ate at a young woman's soul like acid on wood.

Each of the women had perfectly symmetrical features, with flawless skin. Their lips were like something from a lipstick ad, and their eyes were narrowed *just* enough to give them that sultry look most models knew how to conjure at a whim.

Normally, Ella wasn't one quite taken with another's physical appearance. But something about these women...

She continued to stare.

And then realized Brenner was staring too...

A small, niggling part of her subconscious suggested that it was perhaps *Brenner's* attention towards these women that was most troubling to her. But she hated this idea and pushed it aside with a scowl.

Just as quickly, she hid the frown under an impassive, cautious glance.

"Not trying to say anything by it," Brenner said quickly. "Just... you know, maybe that's the connection."

"You think?" she muttered. Her stomach lurched again as the plane continued to descend.

Brenner grinned at her now. It was a rare thing to see the ex Navy sniper smile. But now he flashed it at her and gave an appreciative nod while scratching at the scar under his chin. "Shit. Was that sarcasm, from Ella Porter?"

Ella rolled her eyes but then caught the expression as Brenner rubbed at his chest again.

Her stomach lurched as the plane hit a bout of turbulence. "Coming in for a choppy landing! Hold on to your asses, folks," the captain called over the radio.

Ella tensed even further. To distract herself, and also to assuage her conscience, she whispered, "Are you okay?"

"Huh?"

"Your chest?"

"Fine. Yeah," he said, tight-lipped.

"It still hurts, doesn't it?"

"I've had worse for longer," he shot back. "Shit!" he added as they hit another jolting bump.

His phone, displaying the gorgeous faces of the three murdered goddesses, vanished as it fell from his lap onto the ground.

She couldn't honestly say she was too upset by this.

The plane shook violently as it made its descent, and Ella gripped the armrests tightly, her knuckles turning white. She could feel Brenner's eyes on her, but she refused to look at him. She was afraid that if she did, he would see the fear in her eyes. She hated feeling vulnerable in front of anyone, especially him.

Finally, after what felt like an eternity, the plane touched down on the runway with a loud *thud*. Ella let out a sigh of relief and released her grip on the armrests. She glanced over at Brenner, who was rubbing his chest again.

"Come on," she said, standing up and grabbing her bag from under the cramped seat.

15

Brenner nodded, and together they made their way off the plane and onto the tarmac.

They were met by a black SUV with tinted windows. Ella recognized the driver.

"Who's that?" Brenner muttered.

"What? Oh, Agent Johnson. Works for the Juneau field office."

"You know him?"

"Not personally. We spoke over video last week, though."

Brenner just eyed Johnson, seemingly suspicious.

But the Agent in question was a well-built man with an athletic frame, and despite the cold weather, he only wore a thin t-shirt. His arms were covered in so many tattoos, Ella could barely see the skin.

"H'lo," Johnson called out distractedly, nodding at them both in turn. He opened the door for them and they climbed inside.

"Where to?" Johnson asked, starting the engine.

"The crime scene," Ella said, leaning back in her seat. "I was told you preserved it?"

"Not the body."

"No, I know. But the rest?"

He shrugged, nodding at her in the rearview mirror.

At the man's curt, untalkative nature, Brenner seemed to relax a bit, as if he'd found a kindred soul.

Brenner went quiet beside her, staring out the window at the passing scenery as the car picked up speed.

They were leaving the airport, moving quickly, heading towards the crime scene.

And that's when the tires blew out, and the car skidded off the road.

Chapter 2

Ella's head slammed against the headrest as the vehicle spun off the side of the road, jarring over a culvert.

Her heart raced as she fought to keep her seatbelt secure. The car finally came to a stop with a thud, and for a moment, everything was still. Ella's chest heaved as she tried to catch her breath.

"Everyone okay?" Johnson's voice broke the silence.

Ella glanced over at Brenner, who was rubbing his chest again but otherwise seemed unharmed.

"I'm fine," she said, her voice shaking.

Johnson nodded, taking a deep breath. "I'll go check the damage. Stay put."

Ella watched as he got out of the car and walked around to the front. She couldn't see much from her vantage point, but she could hear the sound of his footsteps crunching in the snow.

Brenner leaned over to her, his voice low. "Are you okay?"

She swallowed hard, nodding. "Yeah. You?"

"I've had worse," he said, his lips quirking up in a half-smile.

Johnson opened the door and climbed back inside. "We're not going anywhere," he said, his voice grim. "Tires are shot."

"Like actually shot?" Brenner said quickly.

"What? Nah. Sorry. Turn of phrase. Glass on the road."

Brenner frowned, unbuckled, and pushed out of the front seat. "Glass?" he muttered. "Glass doesn't puncture..."

He trailed off, moving away from the open door, towards the road. Ella watched him go, through the door, her gaze tracing the gouge marks in the mud left behind where they'd veered off the road.

"What is it?" she called out.

Brenner had dropped to a knee, frowning at the ground. He looked up, shaking his head. "Someone did this on purpose. Come, look."

Ella hesitated, realized Johnson was watching her, and suppressed her frown.

People often thought it was a sign of weakness not to constantly express every errant thought cartwheeling through their minds.

But in Ella's opinion, holding one's tongue was evidence of self-control and self-government.

Plus, she liked to play her cards close to the chest.

19

She was glad she'd worn two layers now, as she moved out onto the side of the road, the airport nearly a half hour from the city perched water-side.

Now, she stared at the ground where Brenner's gloved fingers were brushing pine needles aside and scraping small fragments across the asphalt.

"Not just glass, see?" he said. "Nails. Screws. Shrapnel."

"Shrapnel?"

"Mhmm."

She looked at the ground and realized that the entire roadway was covered with the makeshift tire-shredders.

She paused, frowning, looking up now, and glancing off towards the surrounding trees.

Her heart was picking up pace now, and she swallowed nervously.

Brenner was also looking. His training as a sniper had given him an eye for details which she relied on.

She still remembered her interaction with him back in the hospital room, though.

Well... not quite with *him*.

But her sister.

At the time... she frowned, thinking about what Priscilla had told her. About what Ella had learned.

She shook aside the thought, pushing it away.

More information had come out over the next few weeks whenever she could gather it. But now... she almost wished she hadn't looked.

Things with Brenner were different.

And yet they felt so similar.

He stood there, wearing his brown, leather jacket, rubbing a hand through his thick beard. He wore flannel under the jacket, which she assumed was a requirement for most manly men in Alaska.

And now, he pointed off through the trees. "Someone came from that way. Left an hour or so ago."

Johnson grunted. "I've got backup on its way. Sorry folks."

Ella waved away the apology. Brenner just nodded.

"Welcome to Juneau," Johnson added.

Ella sighed, swallowing. She didn't feel particularly welcome.

They still had a crime scene to visit.

And now someone had intentionally impeded their investigation.

Things were starting to get complicated.

Chapter 3

The backup vehicle brought them to the crime scene of the latest victim, the third in as many weeks, nearly three hours later, and Brenner was already scowling.

He tugged at the edges of his gloves, trying not to limp too heavily on his injured leg. The leg injury was an old one. The chest ache was new.

Still, he strode purposefully forward, following after where Ella Porter set the pace.

She was a good head shorter than him, and hers was a pretty head for sure, but she walked with brusque, determined strides, and only occasionally glanced back.

He found himself watching her, his eyes attentive. She'd been acting strangely around him ever since he'd been shot two months before.

They still hadn't talked about it all... He frowned, closing his eyes briefly, massaging the bridge of his nose, and wishing things had gone differently.

He hadn't talked with Ella about the time he'd had with Priscilla. The child they'd had.

Things with Cilla were over, of course...

They had to be.

Ella was back. And she'd always been his sweetheart. The one who'd been there for him when all he had waiting for him back at home was bruising and bluster on behalf of a drunken man who'd emotionally taxed his own wife into an early grave.

Brenner jammed his hands into his pockets as he frowned, trying to summon some inner courage to address Ella.

They needed to have it out.

He wasn't even sure what they needed to talk about, but he knew things had changed.

And he hated it.

"Right here," said Agent Johnson. The curt, muscled, and well-built FBI operative gestured towards a set of spruce trees at the base of a mountain, near a wildlife trail carving through the wilderness.

Behind them, the all-terrain Jeep had taken them as far as it could, and they'd been walking for the last five minutes to cover the rest of the distance.

At Johnson's declaration, Ella hurried forward, a skip in her step.

Brenner followed at a more leisurely pace. His eyes were on the orange pup tent set up in the copse of trees.

The tent was abandoned.

The nearest tree, above the tent, had branches stripped away, judging by the pale, naked wood along the brown bark.

"This is where the body was found hanging?" Ella asked, glancing back at their guide.

Johnson nodded once. "Arms spread," he said. "Barbed wire."

Ella frowned, turning back to the tree, her eyes fixated on the trunk.

It wasn't the first time they'd found a body near a tree. Brenner stood off to the side, surveying the scene, his eyes on the trees.

Someone had sabotaged their vehicle. Someone had booby-trapped the road leading from the airport.

The killer?

Friends of the killer?

He didn't like being in the open like this. Visible from the mountains. His mind filled with memories of glowing, red, reticles. His sniper rifle braced against his shoulder.

He frowned, blinked, clearing the image from his mind, and turned as Ella declared, "Look here!"

She was gesturing excitedly, standing under the tree but staring at the ground. She looked even more energetic now than when they'd first landed.

Ella wasn't scared of much. Save for the ocean and open water, she was the type to push her fears aside and press to the limits.

She had a history of sky-diving, deep-sea fishing, para-gliding... And those were just the adrenaline-laced sports he'd heard about.

Something about the danger, about channeling her frustrations into the habits of an adrenaline junkie also translated to solving crimes.

As if working with the FBI, pursuing dangerous predators, was her version of an extreme sport.

Not that she didn't care... She was one of the most tender-hearted people he knew.

And now, she was scanning the clearing, moving methodically, meticulously. Her work ethic was rivaled by few, save, perhaps, her twin sister, Cilla.

But Ella left no pine needle unregistered. Her eyes trailed over the ground, moving slowly as she walked around the area.

She glanced back up at the tree where the body had been posed, then at the ground now.

She stopped. Stared.

"What is it?"

She didn't reply, but hesitated, tilting her head.

"Find something?"

Now, she was pointing at the ground, then bending to a knee, her gloved finger scraping aside pine needles.

Brenner approached reluctantly, his eyes still moving along the trees, searching for danger.

"What is it?"

Ella didn't answer immediately. She was too focused on the small, circular object she had uncovered.

Brenner leaned in closer, studying the object. It was a silver locket, intricately carved with a floral design.

His heart dropped as he reached out to take the locket from Ella's hand.

"What is it?" she repeated, looking up at him with concern etched across her face.

Brenner took a deep breath, trying to steady himself before speaking. "The design," he said slowly.

He hesitated, shaking his head, and opening his eyes wide as if to clear them of black spots. He murmured to himself, shivered, and shook his head again.

"What is it?" she repeated, standing up now, hiding the frown he detected in her voice.

She was often good at masking her emotions.

Brenner, on the other hand, had been accused in the past of wearing his heart on his sleeve.

He stared at the twisting floral design and could make out the two eye sockets formed by the rose petals. Out loud he said, "Twelve."

And then he turned the locket over for the first time.

There, in the silver, on the back, was the number twelve.

Ella stared, blinked, then looked up at him.

"What is this?"

"My old team," he said softly. And then he turned, glancing back at where Agent Johnson leaned against the hood of their car. Now it made sense who'd ambushed the road. Someone had wanted to stall them. Someone who'd known what they'd been doing.

"Brenner, you're not making any sense."

He cleared his throat. "A branch of SEAL Team twelve—most people don't know about twelve. That design, a skull made from flowers, was ours."

She wrinkled her nose, her pale blue eyes intent on him now. "I don't believe I understand," she said slowly. "Please help me."

Even now, standing at a murder scene. Please. Mannerly as ever. Ella had been a princess in Nome, born to a gold-mining dynasty.

He'd often felt insecure when compared to her upbringing.

But now, staring at the marking of the familiar symbol on the locket, he shook his head. "It's not a common symbol."

"So you're saying someone from your old SEAL team, an off-the-books, special ops killer, is out here?"

He shrugged. "The victim wasn't. Neither of the witnesses. So who else?"

He turned to look at her, still holding the chain loosely where it dangled over his palm.

Ella was staring at him with a mix of disbelief and curiosity. Brenner could tell she was trying to piece together the implications of what he had just told her. He could see her mind working furiously, trying to make sense of the situation.

"So, what do we do now?" Ella asked, breaking the silence. Her eyes moved slowly around the rest of the crime scene, taking it all in.

Brenner took a deep breath and looked around the area. He couldn't shake the feeling that they were being watched. The hairs on the back of his neck stood up, and he had to fight the urge to draw his weapon.

"We need to find out who this locket belongs to," Brenner said, his voice low and serious. "It could be a clue to the killer's identity. I have some people I can call. Old friends."

Ella nodded, her eyes still on the locket. "Okay, let's go talk to the witnesses again. Maybe they saw something that could help us."

Brenner nodded in agreement, and the two of them made their way back to the car. As they walked, Brenner couldn't shake the feeling that they were being followed. He kept glancing over his shoulder, scanning the trees for any signs of movement.

When they reached the car, Agent Johnson was already inside, his eyes glued to a laptop screen.

"Anything new?" Brenner asked, opening the car door.

Johnson shook his head. "Nothing yet. The local PD is being tight-lipped, and we don't have any solid leads on whoever punctured our tires."

Brenner sighed and took a seat in the back of the car. Ella sat next to him, still holding the locket in her hand. Brenner paused, then said, "I might have an idea about the tires."

The man in the seat glanced back. "Oh?"

"Ex-military," Brenner said simply. "SEAL. Know of anyone like that in the area?"

"Nah. But we have some off-gridders around. A lot of them are frog-men and Marines."

Brenner nodded, frowning. They began to pull away, and he felt his skin prickle in a rising fear. Ella was staring determinedly out the window, a look in her eyes that he'd seen before.

She often got like this, like a bloodhound with the scent of prey.

Her eyes narrowed, and she brushed a lock of golden hair aside.

He found his heart skipping a beat as he watched her, but the excited jolt was accompanied by a pang of longing. And of loss.

Things had changed between them.

But some things never changed—three gorgeous victims killed in the last month meant that Brenner Gunn and Ella Porter were on the trail of another serial killer.

Chapter 4

Ella watched closely as the young couple sat nervously in the police precinct, both of them fidgeting uncomfortably.

She pushed through the door, entering the room, affixing a polite smile to her face.

Brenner followed behind her, slouched and frowning.

"Good evening," Ella said softly, nodding to Gabe and Mary in turn.

The two campers who'd discovered the body kept glancing at the door, swallowing nervously. Gabe's foot tapped rhythmically against the ground. The young man's hair was slicked back as if he'd recently showered, and he wore an orange jacket, designed for warmth but also for visibility, matching the color of the tent he'd set up.

His girlfriend, Mary, had a heart-shaped face, and a nervous smile that caused dimples to form on her cheeks.

The two of them were holding hands under the table, providing some hidden strength through their touch.

Ella didn't sit but remained standing across the table. Not to communicate condescension or authority, but to communicate urgency.

Her smile offset misinterpretation. She was well-studied in the modes of human psychology. In fact, most of her studies had been passed with flying colors.

And now, she could feel a familiar urge rising within her. The same urge that accompanied a soul before jumping from an airplane with a parachute attached to one's back.

Or before diving off a steep cliff into unknown waters. Or at the moment of creaking metal before an underwater cage door was opened, to allow a diver to swim with sharks.

It came as a rush of excitement, tinged with fear, but her skin was buzzing. And her mind zeroed in on the issue at hand.

"I know you've been over this already," Ella said softly, "But I'd like to hear it again, if you don't mind."

Gabe twitched, opened his mouth, closed it. Mary was the one who spoke first. "Who-who are you?"

"Apologies," Ella said. "I'm Agent Porter. This is Marshal Gunn. We're with the FBI and US Marshals service."

"Oh. Okay. Well... we've already told everything we know," Mary said nervously.

"You two were out there for how long?" Ella said.

Mary glanced at her partner. Gabe ran a hand through his already slick hair. "Only a couple hours," he said. "We wanted to see the lights."

"The Northern Lights?"

"Mhmm."

"Did you?"

"They were starting."

Ella hesitated and glanced at Brenner, who shrugged back at her.

"The body was found suspended in a tree, but the victim was still alive, we're told."

"It was horrible," Mary whispered, her voice hoarse.

"She's dead. Right? They said she died on the way to the hospital," Gabe said, his voice shaking.

Ella didn't reply to this question, preferring to ask one of her own. "Did the victim say anything?"

"No... she asked for help, then died," Mary said. Her eyes were wide, her face pale.

Ella felt a jolt of sympathy. She could remember the first time she'd seen someone die. It stuck with her. She kept her tone gentle as she said, "Anything else?"

"Nothing."

"Was the victim wearing a locket?" Brenner said suddenly.

Everyone glanced towards him. Ella nodded faintly at the question. They'd checked with the coroner on the two *earlier* victims, also beautiful women, also found near the icefields over the last month. No lockets there. The coroner was still working on the newest body and would update them when she had any news.

At Brenner's question, they all paused. Mary was staring at her hands. Gabe was frowning now. Brenner seemed to have this effect on some people.

"No," Gabe said at last. "I mean... not that I know of." His puffy, orange jacket sleeves crinkled against the smooth metal table.

"And did you see anyone near the body? See anyone leaving the campsite?" Ella asked.

"No. Nothing like that either," Gabe said. "I... I'm sorry, but it's like we said. We don't know anything. We just saw her there."

"Was the body already there when you set up your tent?" Ella asked.

"It must've been... It's so horrifying to think that. But how else would it have gotten there? It was darker before the lights came out. So... So maybe it was there, and we just didn't see her."

"Or hear her," Mary pointed out. She raised a hand like a child in class. "Can we stop calling her *the body?* She was a person."

Ella nodded once in a sort of acknowledgment but then said, "So is there a chance she was put there after you set up?"

The question lingered. Everyone shivered, frozen in place. "What a terrible thought," Mary whispered.

Gabe shrugged. "It's possible. We were gone from the site for like an hour waiting for the lights."

Ella nodded, crossing her arms and frowning. She needed some angle. Something she hadn't thought of. But it sounded like the two of them really hadn't seen or heard anything.

She paused, considering this, then tried a different question. "Do you know about off-gridders in the area? You two are local, right?"

"I am," Mary said. "He's not. But, I mean, yeah. It's Alaska, after all."

Brenner cut in. "Do you know of any with military backgrounds?"

"I mean, sure... I don't know them personally. Why?"

"No reason." Then, deciding this was too cold, Brenner said, "One of our victims had a locket near her which matched an old SEAL team's emblem. Another victim's father was military."

Ella glanced over. She hadn't remembered that part of the background profiles of the first two victims. She'd already gone through their details meticulously. Three victims so far, but the first two had been killed weeks before. The freshest clue, though it felt callous to think of it in such a way, was the body in the trees.

Ella noticed the way Mary was looking at Brenner, her eyes narrowing. "Why do you ask?" she said.

"We're just trying to gather as much information as possible," Ella said calmly. "Anything you can tell us, no matter how small, might be helpful."

Mary seemed to consider this for a moment, then said, "There's a guy who lives off the grid near here. I don't know him, but I've heard stories about him. They say he was in the military."

"What kind of stories?" Brenner asked.

Mary shrugged. "Just that he's... I don't know... weird. Keeps to himself. Hunts a lot. People say he's got a temper."

Ella exchanged a glance with Brenner. It wasn't much to go on, but it was something. "Do you know where we could find this guy?" she asked.

Mary hesitated. "I mean, I don't know exactly where he is. But I could show you the general area on GPS."

"That would be helpful," Ella said, pulling out her phone.

Gabe looked like he wanted to say something else, but Mary was already standing as well. "Yeah, no problem. Anything to help."

She leaned in as Ella extended her phone, showing a map of the area. She tapped a finger against the screen. "His house is here. No address, just in the trees."

"He lives alone?"

"No... No, there's like a community of these guys."

"Know his name?" Brenner said, his voice tense.

"Don't think so. We just call him Wildman."

"Wildman. Great."

Mary was now tugging at her boyfriend's arm, leading him to the door. He paused, opened his mouth again, and then said quickly, "Do you know why someone would do that? Why... why anyone would..." he trailed off, a haunted look in his eyes.

Ella knew that look. She felt a pang of sadness on behalf of Mary and Gabe. They'd seen too much at their tender age.

Ella just shook her head. "We'll find them. I promise."

As she looked at Mary, she was briefly reminded of her younger cousin, Maddie.

Deciding this wasn't enough, Ella added, "Don't worry. You're safe."

"I wasn't worried," Mary said. "It's just... so *wrong*." Shaking her head, she turned and led her boyfriend out of the room, leaving Ella and Brenner watching after them.

Once the door clicked shut, Ella turned to Brenner.

"So, what do you think?" she asked, folding her arms across her chest.

Brenner leaned back, his eyes closed, face towards the ceiling. "I think we need to find this Wildman. But I don't remember anyone named that on one of the teams..."

"Mary said there were others with him in the area. Might be one of them?"

"Yeah... Possibly. We also need to be careful. If he's ex-military, then he's dangerous."

"We'll be careful," Ella said.

Brenner frowned at her as the two of them turned towards the door.

"What?" she said.

"The way you said that... I hate that you *like* the danger."

"I do *not*."

"You do. You just won't admit it. Come on. Let's go."

Brenner pushed out of the room, and Ella frowned as she followed quickly after him.

Chapter 5

Laura moved up the mountain trail, her breath puffing with each step, but her eyes were fixed on the icefields ahead.

Just outside Juneau, serving as the passage for over thirty glaciers, the icefields were a sight to behold, especially at night with the dancing lights from the northern skies streaking the cold crystals.

Laura moved with long strides, keeping her heart rate up. She glanced at her fitness watch, making sure she was still sticking to her goals.

Twenty-thousand steps a day. No matter what.

One wasn't able to maintain *this* physique without effort.

She wore goggles covering her face, protecting her features from the elements. It wasn't usual for her to hide her visage—in fact, it paid most of her bills.

But the blistering cold, the elements could cause damage to her complexion, so she'd made sure to wear a protective covering.

"Just another step," Laura murmured to herself, her lips stinging from the cold. She'd need to apply a new layer of ChapStick soon. "Just another step."

She reached the plateau, looking out at the icefields. Behind her, far below, she spotted where her boyfriend had dropped her off via snowmobile.

He hadn't wanted to join her for the hike.

She sniffed, frowning over her shoulder, and wondering if it was time to trade in for a newer model.

She returned her attention to the icefields, though, her eyes widening.

The green and blue hues of the night sky were starting to dance, like fairies flitting to some unheard music.

Laura gasped as she watched the colors swirl and twist, mesmerized by the beauty of the aurora borealis.

As she stood there, lost in thought, she heard a faint noise.

The crack of ice.

She turned sharply, glancing back.

And stiffened. Her heart skipped a beat. Another. Her breath caught in her throat.

A man was standing a few feet away, watching the northern lights with her. He wore a hood low over his face.

"Jeremy?" she said slowly, frowning. But no... no, this wasn't her boyfriend's jacket.

Her heart continued to pound.

She was alone. Isolated out here in the evening.

No one for miles. The city in the distance, at sea level, serving as a lighthouse, the glow from the buildings like a beacon.

But far too distant to be of any aid.

She was alone.

Where had the man come from? She hadn't seen him on the trail.

He didn't glance at her but instead stood rocking on his heels, hands behind his back, staring at the mesmerizing sight.

"Beautiful, isn't it?" he said, his voice deep and smooth.

Laura nodded, unable to take her eyes off him. Should she run? H e... he sounded friendly enough. Where the hell had he come from, though?

She was flustered, and her mind was spinning. She tried to reorient and let out a faint, shuddering breath. She began to inch away, back towards the trail.

He didn't move to intercept.

Maybe he was just another hiker who'd come for the same sight.

Maybe he had been here first.

As if reading her mind, he glanced at her, from under his hood. "I come up here often," he said, stepping closer to her. "It's my favorite spot to watch the lights."

Laura tried to force a smile, feeling a shiver run down her spine. She wasn't sure what it was about this man, but she couldn't deny the eerie prickle along her spine. Something in his voice. In his posture.

It was the confidence, she realized.

Sheer, unadulterated confidence that *he* was in complete control.

She took another half step towards the trailhead. The beautiful sight, the fields of ice, were all forgotten now.

Her fear was rising.

The man didn't glance at her now, instead standing stock still, his hands still clasped behind his back as he rocked on his heels.

They remained there in silence for a few moments, watching the colors dance in the sky as Laura tried to inch away.

She reached the top of the descending incline, steadying her foot on a slick patch of ground.

Suddenly, moving so fast it caused her to gasp, he turned to her and said, "My name is Nikolai. And you are?"

"Laura," she replied, her voice barely above a whisper. "I... sorry... my boyfriend is just... just down there. He's umm... Hi, Grant!" she called, waving off to nowhere.

It was a thin, pathetic attempt.

Nikolai smiled, his eyes twinkling in the light under his hood. "Well, Laura, it's nice to meet you. But isn't your boyfriend's name Jeremy?"

She froze. "Umm... Do—do I know you?" Was this a prank? A joke? Had Jeremy put one of his model friends up to it? The asshole.

She could feel anger rising.

He was still so calm, so confident as he said, "It really is quite beautiful. A natural beauty. *True* beauty. None of this fake vanity we see around us so often. Isn't that right?" He looked fully at her now, his gaze like a needle, as if piercing the wings of a butterfly.

She felt affixed to the spot. And her terror continued to course through her.

"Umm... I really need to go. My boyfriend is waiting for me."

"No, he isn't."

Confident again. No hesitation. This man *knew*. Knew her boyfriend's name. Knew her?

She'd heard enough. His creepy schtick had ruined the trip up the mountain.

She turned and began to move, walking briskly back down the trail.

"Don't go," he said simply.

It wasn't a request.

She began to move faster.

"I told you to stay!" he called over his shoulder, still watching the lights.

She ignored him now, panic and adrenaline fueling her motions. She broke into a jog, racing hastily down the trail now.

She glanced back, and he was still standing there, like a statue. She'd put fifty feet between them. A hundred.

Maybe she was fine. She found relief returning.

He wasn't moving.

She began to turn down the switchback...

And then caught the blur of motion.

One moment, he'd been standing still, motionless.

The next, he spun and stared at her, his eyes widening beneath his hood, his mouth following. He screamed, "I told you not to *leave*!"

And then he broke into a dead sprint, racing after her.

Her own scream shook the icefields as she fled, desperately trying to escape the stranger.

Chapter 6

Ella moved through the trees ahead of Brenner, the two of them wearing jackets against the night-time cold.

Darkness had fallen completely, and the night sky was sparkling with stars. Brenner was moving slower but keeping his eyes on the tree line, the two of them following the GPS coordinates they'd been given in order to locate the off-grid commune.

"Psst, there," Brenner said suddenly, pointing through the trees.

The two of them went still, listening to the sound of the cold, Alaskan night.

The wind whispered through dark foliage, and swirling ice crystals lifted off the ground, swept like mist across the forest floor before falling once again.

In the distance, the flicker of light off the icefields cast the landscape in a bluish sheen.

Through the trees, Ella spotted a wooden structure. She stared at it, eyes narrowed.

And then she spotted movement.

She glanced sharply at Brenner to see if he'd spotted it as well, but he was already nodding, holding up two fingers, and pointing towards the trees.

Another figure, this one leaning against a trunk. She hadn't spotted him at first.

Brenner's eyes were more accustomed to picking out targets in camouflaged terrain.

Now, the two of them moved silently through the woods, stepping amidst the trees, across the sparse ground cover, into the space.

They passed a hand-painted sign, which looked to have been made out of the blood from the creature whose antlers were piercing it to the trunk. The message was simple.

No Trespassers.

And there were bullet holes riddling the white laminate background.

They were here to find a man simply known as Wildman. Someone, Brenner suggested, who'd once been a Navy SEAL himself.

Brenner's weapon was tight in his hand. Her own hand hovered near her holster.

As they approached the wooden structure, Ella's senses were on high alert. She could hear the sound of muffled voices and the occasional clink of metal coming from within. Brenner signaled to her to take the right while he took the left. They crept forward, their footsteps light against the hard ground.

Ella hugged the wall as she stepped towards the entrance, her heart skipping in her chest. She could see the flickering shadows on the walls as she approached. She could hear the low murmur of voices coming from inside, but she couldn't make out what they were saying. She reached for her gun, feeling the cold metal in her hand, and took a deep breath to steady herself.

Brenner was already at the doorway, his gun drawn and ready. He glanced back at Ella, nodding his head to indicate that he was ready.

Suddenly the door creaked open, and a shadowy figure appeared.

"Who are you?" the figure demanded, brandishing a rifle.

Ella stepped forward, her own weapon at the ready.

Brenner was off to her side.

"FBI!" Ella said firmly. "FBI! Lower your rifle!"

The man didn't.

He looked like a cross between a grizzly bear and a refrigerator. Easily twice the size of most men, the giant's chest puffed out well past his chin.

Behind him, Ella quickly glanced inside the wooden structure; the air was thick with smoke from a fire burning in the fireplace. Several men were sitting around a table playing poker, while others lounged on couches and chairs. They all turned to look at Ella and Brenner, staring at them through the door.

At least five men.

All of them armed.

Shit, she thought, standing in place.

She swallowed and called a bit louder, "FBI! Stay where you are. I'm Agent Porter. Please keep your hands where I can see them!"

"We're here to talk to Wildman," Brenner said, his voice low and steady, interjecting from where he stood out of line of sight.

The men within the cabin exchanged looks before one of them stood up, frowning. He had a revolver jammed into the front of his belt.

The hairy giant in the doorway, though, was glaring at the two of them.

His rifle was beginning to lower ever so slightly, and Ella could feel her anxiety rising.

Adrenaline coursed through her veins.

"Drop the weapon!" Brenner said.

His tone was one of calm, confidence. his hand didn't waver as he pointed the weapon at their aggressor. The other men inside the cabin were now rising, frowning. The two sentries they'd spotted earlier were stalking over, footsteps crunching on leaves and debris.

"FBI!" Ella kept repeating, her voice hoarse. "Don't move!"

"We don't recognize you, here," said the big man in the door.

He took a step closer, snarling. His face was half beard and half scowl.

He straightened his hunched shoulders, having squeezed through the doorway, and Ella realized just *how* big he was.

His rifle was now aiming towards the ground at Brenner's feet. But his hands were twitching.

The men inside the cabin were twitching.

"Where's Wildman?" Snapped Brenner, displaying no fear.

"I'm Wildman," snarled the giant.

Brenner sized him up, then snorted. "No way you were a SEAL."

"Who said Wildman was a SEAL?" called the voice of the man with the revolver in his belt.

This fellow was older than the others, with salt-and-pepper hair and wire-frame glasses. He looked bookish, in a way, but his hands were weather-worn, and his boots were caked in a thin layer of mud.

Ella's eyes had fixated on this man in particular. She didn't believe the giant was the military man they were looking for.

She reached into her pocket, carefully, and pulled out the silver locket with the flower-skull they'd found at the crime scene.

"Anyone recognize this?" she called out, holding the item up. She watched their reactions closely.

No one blinked. No recognition in anyone's eyes.

The two sentries had come to a stop behind Ella and Brenner. The five men inside the cabin were now all on their feet.

It took everything in her not to turn tail and run.

"Don't recognize it," said the giant with the rifle. "Now scram. This is Alaska. Trespassers are dealt with personal like." He had a slow, lumbering way of moving which matched his speech patterns.

He took a step towards Brenner and tapped the marshal's shoe with the barrel of his rifle.

Brenner didn't step back, his hand gripping his own gun. "We're not leaving until we get some answers," he said firmly. "We're investigating a murder, and you. Tap my foot again, and I'll knock you out."

Brenner said it matter-of-factly, and the giant, with arms as large as Ella's abdomen, snorted as if he'd heard some good joke.

The men in the cabin exchanged looks, and the giant's scowl deepened. "We don't know anything about no murder," he growled. "I told you to scram!"

Ella wasn't convinced, but she could tell tensions were reaching a boiling point. She took a step forward, holding out the locket. "This was found at the scene," she said. "It belongs to someone here." She didn't know this, but she said it confidently, again watching reactions.

But there were none.

Everyone just stared at her, frowning.

Wildman's eyes narrowed as he suddenly reached out and snatched the locket from her. He examined it for a moment, his thick fingers tracing the skull made of flowers and the number twelve on the back. "I don't know who this belongs to," he said finally. "But I can tell you we don't take kindly to people snooping around here." He tossed the locket back at her, and it bounced off her chest, falling to the ground with a silver flash.

There was a tense moment of silence as the men in the cabin regarded her, their faces inscrutable. Then, the man with the revolver made his final mistake.

Ella could already tell Brenner was losing his temper. But the moment the man tossed the locket at her, he also tapped at Brenner with his rifle again.

"Now," the big guy said. "I told you to—"

Brenner didn't speak. He didn't say something cheesy like *I warned you*. He didn't allow the giant to know the blow was coming.

Brenner wasn't a fighter—or a boxer.

He had been trained to *end* fights, not engage in them.

And so the moment the rifle tapped his foot a second time, Brenner moved with lightning speed.

Fast and merciless, one hand shot out and caught the giant's tender throat, a thumb jamming hard into his larynx. A knee came up second, slamming into the giant's crotch, and a final punch caught the man in the solar plexus.

All of it happened in half a second, faster than anyone could react.

And by the time the giant's gurgle of pain and gasp of air was registered by the others in the cabin, Brenner was already stepping back, the rifle in his hand now, pointed into the cabin, his own weapon somehow having been simultaneously holstered in the excitement.

"Don't move," Brenner said coolly. And he wasn't breathing heavily. "You two," he added, waving at the sentries, "Join your friends inside. Bit too cold out here for you."

The two guards who'd been roaming the trees exchanged uncomfortable looks but shifted past the FBI agent and the Marshal, stepping over the groaning, gurgling form of their doorman.

As the sentries disappeared inside the cabin, Brenner motioned for Ella to follow him. They cautiously stepped over the giant's body, making their way inside. The cabin was dark, with walls made of rough-hewn wood and a small fire flickering in the corner. The air was thick with the scent of woodsmoke and sweat.

The men inside were tense, watching them with narrowed eyes as they entered. The man with the revolver was still standing, his hand on his gun. Ella could see the suspicion in his eyes as he regarded Brenner. But there was no fear.

"We're not here to cause trouble," Brenner said, his voice calm. "We're here to find out what happened to a young woman only a few miles from here."

There was a moment of silence as the men looked at each other. Ella could feel sweat prickling inside her palms.

Finally, the man with the revolver spoke up. "We don't know anything about a murder," he said, his voice steady. "We've been up here for years, just trying to get away from it all. Why would we shit where we eat? We don't hurt women or children."

Ella wondered if this meant they saw no problem with hurting men. But she decided not to point out the oversight in vernacular.

Brenner regarded the man for a moment, then nodded. "I believe you," he said. "But we still need to ask a few questions. You're Wildman?"

The man with the revolver hesitated, then nodded once. "Some call me that. You can call me Jake. You military?"

Brenner nodded.

"Frogman?"

Brenner nodded again. "You a Green Beret?"

The man named Wildman shrugged. "Once upon a time. Quite a while ago." He ran his hand through his graying hair.

The other men in the room seemed to relax a bit as this gray-haired fellow seemed to maintain his calm.

Though occasionally, they would glance to the giant still groaning on the ground and shoot angry looks at Brenner. One man in particular, standing in the back with shadows wreathing his face, was glowering out at them like some demon wreathed in smoke.

This man had pitch-black hair and a beard to match. His eyes were a piercing green like verdant foliage.

Ella kept glancing at this man, keeping her eye on him as she listened to Brenner.

The marshal was saying, "You got any marks on your recent movements?"

Wildman shrugged. "Been around here mostly. With the boys. We like it out in the woods."

Brenner crossed his arms. He nodded back at Ella and said, "That locket. You ever seen it before?"

"No. Can't say I have."

"Know the emblem?"

"The twelfth team?"

"Mhmm."

Wildman shrugged. "Heard of it. Don't know anyone in it. Except maybe yourself, right?"

Brenner didn't reply to this guess. Instead, he glanced around the small space once more, waving a hand briefly to clear where smoke was whirling towards him. He then shrugged and glanced back at Ella.

For her part, she was frowning. They'd come here on the locket clue. Hoping to find a military-type. But Brenner's clue suggested that the killer was an ex-SEAL. Not a Green Beret.

And now, standing here, looking at the group, she considered their options. Arresting the lot of them would require backup and time.

So far, they hadn't done anything criminal. At least... not that she was aware of.

She tensed, biting her lip, considering her options.

A Green Beret... not a SEAL. No connection to the victims except for proximity. But everyone up here in Juneau was close to *someone.* The icefields were within sight of most of the isolated roadways.

Besides, Wildman didn't seem that wild at all but reserved.

They had no reason to suspect him. That was the main issue. Nothing tying him to the case. Nothing except the hunch that an ex-military member was involved.

"We should probably get going," she began to say, glancing at Brenner.

But before the words left her lips fully, her phone began to ring. A second later, Brenner's own phone joined in, creating a trilling sound in the cabin.

Frowning, Ella pulled the device from her pocket, pressing it to her ear.

A pause. She listened.

"Agent Porter?"

"Yes," she said, sharing a quick, concerned look with Brenner.

"Yes, sorry for bothering you, ma'am, at this late hour. But we need you," said the grim voice of the operator. "We've found another body."

Chapter 7

The dead of night, well past midnight, found Ella and Brenner moving through the icefields of Juneau, the birthplace of glaciers. The ice glowed a cold blue, and Ella shivered, standing on the windswept ground. Her eyes, however, weren't fixated on the Northern lights sparkling above. The lights didn't usually appear for so long, often only coming for a few minutes before disappearing again.

Now, though, they danced and wove their tapestry across the night sky, under the stars.

And all of it served to highlight the corpse.

It hung from a metal fence post, arms outstretched. Strangely, Ella's eyes lingered on the steel post, as if she couldn't quite bring herself to stare full-on at the corpse.

The pole was streaked in rust, and angled to the side, showing evidence of twisted, metal, mesh wire used to secure a portion of the icefields from interlopers. Signs read *Caution!* or *Danger!*

Above those signs and set against the backdrop of the natural beauty and resplendent sky, Laura Donelly's body dangled like a scarecrow, dripping blood onto the pristine white floor one crimson tap at a time.

Ella shivered, staring at the woman's cold, lifeless features. Wire wrapped around her arms, spreading them out at her sides.

Her face was turned up as if to stare at...

The lights?

Ella looked up as well, watching as greens and blues flashed in the sky.

She frowned. The lights...

What if there was something about *the lights*?

She shivered briefly, still standing there. Brenner came up next to her, nudging her and nodding off to the side.

She glanced back, her eyes temporarily adjusting to the flashing red of emergency vehicles. Police were extending hands towards a small gathering of figures attempting to hold the crowd at bay.

"Who are they?" Ella asked.

"Locals. People from the area. Hikers."

"Why are they here?"

"Heard about the murder. Laura is apparently something of a local celebrity. A model."

"A model?"

"Another beautiful woman."

Ella frowned, shaking her head, her fingers lightly touching against her unpierced ear, feeling the numbness from the cold.

She spotted a familiar figure in the group, watching them. A man standing in the back.

The same man who'd been in the cabin, wreathed in smoke. Now, out here, under the Northern Lights, he cut a less intimidating figure.

His hair was still pitch black, and his features were turned into a faint frown as he watched them. He wasn't staring at the body but, rather, seemed to be keeping an eye on Ella and Brenner.

She frowned, shivered, and looked away.

Brenner was now moving towards the corpse, pausing to glance up. "Would've taken him some time to get her up there," he said.

"Strong then. The wire?"

"Yeah, barbed wire. Same as the other scenes."

"What about cause of death?"

"Stabbed. Same as the others."

Ella shook her head, looking away. She spotted something off to the side of the trail, near the icefields. A sweater lying on the ground. She approached the discarded piece of clothing, bent over, and lifted it.

She glanced at the sweater, then at the victim, frowning. Was it Laura's? She was only wearing a T-shirt. Her jacket was missing.

The sweater lay on the ground... as if the killer had intentionally stripped layers away.

For what reason, though?

She lifted the sweater, waving it back at Brenner. He nodded.

Suddenly, a commotion erupted from the figures gathered by the emergency vehicles.

A cop was wrestling with the dark-haired, brooding man, fighting over a phone.

"I can take pictures! It's a free country!" the man was yelling. "Let go of me! Let go!"

Ella turned, watching.

Brenner shook his head.

She paused and glanced back at the body once more. The cop snatched the phone from the man and waved it at him as if shaking a finger in a scolding motion.

"What is it?" Brenner said, studying the side of her face which was illuminated by the glowing sky.

"Just..." She paused, trailing off, glancing back at the small gathering of people.

Even this late at night, in this isolated place, the people on the outskirts of the icefields had come to witness the spectacle.

And that's what it was, wasn't it?

Spectacle.

"It's... he's killing models."

"Yeah, so?"

"Look at the body."

"Mhmm?"

"No. Don't look at it as a body. Put away your disgust, your anger. Just look."

She was now standing back, staring at the scene before her.

Brenner did the same, raising a quizzical eyebrow.

"What do you see?" she murmured.

"Umm... A corpse?"

"Look broader."

"I see... The Northern Lights... Stars. Ice. Snow."

"Mountains..."

"Yeah, those too."

"And a beautiful model."

He looked at her now, frowning. "What are you getting at?"

"Someone's posing them."

"Right. The killer."

"No. I mean someone's framing them in a pose. There's foreground, middle ground, background. The lighting is intentional. The setting and backdrop are chosen specifically."

Brenner looked back at the corpse, eyebrows rising on his head.

"What's your point."

She looked back at where still others were attempting to sneak pictures of the crime scene.

"He's creating pictures," she said softly.

"I don't understand."

"He's acting like an artist."

Brenner didn't speak now, preferring to watch her shrewdly.

Her mind was so distracted, she'd missed it. The last three bodies had all been beautiful as well. Posed similarly. And now?

Now...

She shook her head. Her mind kept moving back to the small USB drive she'd taken. The journal she'd found. Her father's involvement. The Collective—a group of dangerous killers, according to her sister.

Her thoughts moved to the Graveyard Killer—a skeleton in her own closet; to what she'd heard Priscilla say in that hospital room with Brenner.

But all of that was pushed aside.

She focused on the scene at hand.

It made sense now.

Something clicked into place.

"An artist paints for others just as much as himself," she said. "He wants to share his artwork with the world."

"How does that help us?"

"I... I don't know yet," she said, feeling a temporary jolt of discouragement. But then she nodded. "But we can find out."

Brenner stifled a yawn, nodding as well. He'd booked the hotel they'd be staying at.

And Ella had to admit, despite her desire to keep pushing, exhaustion was taking its toll.

But the killer was communicating something.

Ella just had to find out *what*.

Chapter 8

The hotel in Juneau overlooked the water, and Ella stared through the window of her bedroom, frowning at the choppy seas.

Despite her hatred of all things oceanic, her mind was still spinning with the possibilities of the case.

In one hand, her phone illuminated, glowing off the window glass with a bluish tinge as she overlooked the city.

She glanced down at her search results.

Girl. Dead. Northern Lights.

Another search. *Model. Eyes closed. Alaska.*

She'd tried a variation of searches over the last hour after checking into the hotel, but none had borne fruit just yet.

She sighed, her breath creating a thin layer of mist on the window which she wiped away with the back of her hand.

She heard movement in the room next to her.

Brenner.

He couldn't sleep either.

She nibbled on the corner of her lip, hoping the brief spurt of pain might jog her senses.

She needed to sleep, to think straight.

But now, her mind was moving next door.

She turned, staring at the wall between them. Brenner and Cilla had been together.

Her sister had told her in the hospital.

Not only that...

Ella glanced at the text message Cilla had sent a month ago.

I still care for him. We had a child—and lost a child—together. Hands off.

Ella frowned at the text shaking her head.

She hadn't confronted Brenner about any of it. Hadn't felt right.

He'd been shot two months ago, after all. She'd thought he was going to die.

But every time she went to delete the message from her sister, she hadn't been able to bring herself to do it.

Brenner and Priscilla. Not just together, but... but in love? They'd had a child?

Lost a child?

Brenner was a handsome man, but his eyes were sad. She'd thought the sadness was mostly due to his time with the SEALs.

As she thought about it, she wondered how many times he'd tried to tell her the full extent of all of it.

Had he tried at all?

Her anger flared now. She scowled, her hand bunching around her phone.

He'd been the one to accuse *her* of being a liar. But now the truth came out.

He'd been lying.

Keeping it to himself!

She felt her anger flare again. Her eyes were bleary from lack of sleep. Her heart thumped wildly in her chest.

She could feel her frustration mounting, and then, without a glance back, she marched to the door, stepped into the hall, and approached the door next to her.

Her hand was balled in a fist hovering an inch from the wood. Her face was twisted into a scowl.

But she caught herself.

Patient. Infinitely patient.

Stubborn with a smile but never willing to rock the boat.

She lingered, her hand still caught in the air. Her mind moving to all those times Brenner and her had spent time together in their teenage years.

He'd been there for her when she'd needed an escape from her family.

And she'd done the same for him.

Priscilla *said* things. It didn't mean it was all true, did it?

Maybe she was just screwing with them like she so often did?

No... No, this was different.

The Collective was another one of these things. The USB drive, the small journal... It had all led to a revelation.

Her father was deeply involved.

One of his staff members had been as well.

A local news woman had turned killer, hunting couples and dropping them off the sides of crabbing vessels.

Ella had nearly died tangling with the killer, but it all came back to the Collective. Some secret coalition of serial killers that operated in the nation.

It sounded bizarre. Like something out of a billionaire's fantasy.

But no... no Cilla had told the truth then, too, and Ella still wasn't sure what to do about it.

She could think of *one* person who might know. But she'd sworn off ever communicating with him again.

Now, as her mind moved, it seemed to calm her, serving like exercise for her soul, keeping her stable and relaxed.

She let out a long, lingering breath, closing her eyes as she did, and lowering her hand.

Her anger was still there. Her frustration still lingered, but she didn't have to confront him.

Not tonight.

She was in the middle of turning to move back to her room when Brenner's door flung open.

Ella jumped, startled by the sudden movement. Brenner stood in the doorway, his eyes wide with surprise.

"Ella? What are you doing out here?" he asked.

She hesitated for a moment before responding. "I couldn't sleep. I thought you were awake too."

Brenner nodded slowly, his eyes scanning her face. "You look upset."

Ella's eyes flashed with anger, but she quickly pushed it down, not wanting to start a fight. "I'm fine. Just restless."

Brenner studied her for a moment longer before stepping back into his room. "Do you want to come in?"

Ella hesitated, unsure if she wanted to be alone with him. But she found herself nodding, following him into the room.

It was dark inside, the only light coming from a small lamp on the bedside table. Brenner sat down on the edge of the bed, patting the space next to him.

Ella hesitated for a moment but then sat down next to him. They sat in silence for a few moments, the only sound the gentle lapping of the waves outside.

Finally, Brenner spoke. "What's going on, Ella? You can tell me."

Ella took a deep breath, trying to steady her emotions. "It's just... things with Cilla. And you."

Brenner's eyebrows furrowed in confusion. "What about me?"

Ella hesitated, unsure of how to proceed. But she was here, wasn't she? What was the point in holding back? And so she said, "Cilla said that you two had been together. And that you had a child... and lost a child together."

Brenner's face fell, his eyes searching hers. "She told you all of that?"

Ella nodded, feeling a lump forming in her throat. "And... she said she still cared for you."

Brenner sighed, running a hand through his hair; his finger trailed along his scar under his chin. "Look, Ella, I know this is all a lot to take in. But it's complicated. Cilla and I... it was a long time ago."

"And the child?" she said, finding herself strangely calm.

Brenner looked away, going quiet all of a sudden, the tall man hunched on the edge of his bed, his thin, white T-shirt standing out against his muscled and scarred frame.

Ella felt a pang of sympathy for him. She couldn't imagine what it would be like to lose a child. "I'm sorry, Brenner. I didn't know."

He didn't reply, but just shook his head.

He looked so sad, staring at the ground, his hands clasped in his lap.

She remembered other times he'd adopted the same posture. Once when he'd lost his mother.

"We've been through so much together," Ella said softly.

"Yeah."

"And... and you were with my sister."

He looked at her, his eyes pained. "It was always supposed to be you... She was just... I shouldn't have, but you were gone for years and..." He trailed off again, shaking his head and shrugging as if he knew it was pointless.

"I understand," he said at last, letting out a long sigh. He leaned back, staring at the ceiling, his hands folded now. The hands of a killer, of a shooter. The hands she'd held when they'd been far more tender and gentle, years ago.

"Understand?" she said.

He nodded. "I understand there's no future for us. Because of what I did. I regret it. It caused more pain than I could've imagined. But I was just so... lonely at the time."

He shook his head, eyes closed now. She glanced surreptitiously towards the mini-fridge. Brenner hadn't been drinking in months, but it had always been an issue for him.

But he didn't smell like alcohol. And there was no evidence he'd partaken.

Perhaps it was the late hour or just exhaustion. He didn't normally share his feelings, but she felt some of her anger depleting now.

She hesitated. She knew she was at a branching path. Down one road, accusation. Part of her was angry. Part of her wanted to yell at him. He'd been with Cilla. He'd *chosen* her over Ella.

But another part of her felt this was unfair. She was the one who'd left, hadn't she?

Brenner didn't have a family. She'd left to escape hers. But Brenner's mother had died. He had no siblings, and his father beat him.

Ella had fled.

A branching path. Two choices.

She wasn't sure what she wanted to choose. But then, her heart made the choice for her.

Staring at the side of Brenner's face, tracing the outline of his sculpted features, she couldn't look away.

He was the same young man she'd known all those years ago. Sadder now, but just as loyal, just as kind, just as fierce in the defense of the helpless. Just as blunt. Just as dangerous. Just as...

"I'm sorry," she said.

He blinked, then glanced at her as if confused.

"I'm really sorry for leaving," she whispered.

He stared at her now.

"I shouldn't have. I was the only friend you had. You needed me. And I needed you."

He swallowed. "You don't have to—"

"I'm not. It's true."

He continued to watch her. She gave a faint sniff, nodding now. "I wish... I wish it wasn't like that. Really. I should've stayed. I just couldn't stand *them*. I know Cilla has her ways. I know she pretended to be me that first time. I wish you hadn't been with her. But... look me in the eye."

He did. Icy blue meeting dark hazel.

The two of them stared at each other, sitting on the edge of the bed. The sound of the waves outside didn't reach her ears anymore. She couldn't hear the churning of the heating unit. Or even the sound of the running shower upstairs.

She could only hear Brenner's slow breathing. In-out.

"Do you still care for her?"

He held her gaze. Shook his head a single time. "I swear on everything I care about... I swear on *you*. I never did care for her. She was the closest to you I could have. I know that makes me a bad man. I should've told her that. We both knew we were using the other." He shrugged, finally looking away as if he couldn't bear the shame of holding her gaze any longer.

"Promise me."

"I promise."

"So you... you still care for me?" she said.

Ella was off-script now. She could *hear* herself speaking but couldn't quite compute what she was saying. Her emotions were taking over.

Love... Love wasn't an emotion.

It was a verb.

Love was sacrifice. Commitment. Loyalty. Kindness. Forgiveness. Long-suffering. Love was something that endured trials and pain. Love endured hardship.

Love wasn't about twitterpated feelings or butterflies.

But with Brenner...

She had the emotions too.

How often had he come to her aid? How often had he put himself in harm's way?

He'd suffered when she'd left.

"I'm here now," she said with a whisper.

And for a moment, it felt like the times she would stand on the edge of a cliff, looking down at the mountain pass before taking a leap. Or like the moment right before diving from an airplane. Or right before encountering a serial killer in their lair.

The adrenaline rushed through her. Excitement flared in her chest.

"So what are you going to do about it?" she whispered.

Brenner looked over at her now. He looked surprised if anything. "You and I..." he trailed off, his eyes searching hers.

Ella felt her heart beating faster in her chest. She knew what he was trying to say. "Brenner, I..."

But before she could finish, he leaned in and pressed his lips to hers. She felt a jolt of electricity shoot through her body, and she responded eagerly, deepening the kiss.

They broke apart after a few moments, both gasping for breath. Brenner looked at her, his eyes full of emotion. "I've wanted to do that for a long time, Ella."

Ella smiled, feeling a warmth spreading.

"I've wanted it too, Brenner," she said. "I just didn't know if you felt the same way."

He chuckled, shaking his head. "I've always felt the same way. I just didn't know how to tell you." He was still so close, his breath warm on her face.

She was off-script, but it felt right. No... not *right*. Good. Pleasurable. It was her choice.

Cilla wanted Brenner. Cilla wanted *everything*. But Ella was done with it.

Things were different. She didn't know about the Collective, didn't know how she'd go hunting them down.

Didn't know what her father was into. Didn't know what games were being played.

But Brenner had been hers since she'd been sixteen.

She'd made the mistake in leaving once.

Now she was back.

She'd chosen the path on the branching road.

And it felt so right.

Ella leaned in and kissed him again, feeling the passion building between them. She knew that there were still obstacles to overcome, but for now, she was content to be in his arms.

As they broke apart again, Brenner looked at her, his eyes serious. "Ella, I promise you that I will never hurt you again. I will do everything in my power to make you happy."

Ella smiled, feeling tears prick at the corners of her eyes. She wasn't even sure *why*.

Some emotion, long suppressed. She thought of how she'd felt, half-naked by a fire in the cold, a polar bear chasing them.

Brenner had been there then as well.

He'd literally jumped off a cliff to protect her.

She paused, wondering if now it was up to her to protect him. From heartache. From danger... She had enemies. Her family would keep coming. Cilla would try and make them suffer.

But no.

No, she decided.

She'd made her choice.

"No," she said softly.

"What?"

"Don't promise that." "Promise what?" he said, his eyes half closed, his breath still warm against her cheek.

"That you'll make me happy. That you'll never hurt me again. It's not true. It's not your job to make me happy."

He stared at her, perplexed.

She smiled back. "Hurt happens. I trust you. Just..."

She leaned in again, and it was as if nothing else in the world mattered at all. Their lips pressed against each other.

There was still a killer beneath the Northern Lights. Still danger in Juneau.

And in the morning, it would come rushing back.

But for now, Ella was blissfully ignorant, forgetting everything as she leaned against the only man she'd ever loved.

Chapter 9

Morning came with Ella sitting at the wooden table, her fingers tapping against the keyboard on her computer, and her excitement was mounting.

"I knew it," she whispered. "Yes! I knew it!" she repeated.

She said it quietly, to herself, not wanting to disturb Brenner who was still sleeping on the bed they'd shared.

They hadn't done anything together. At least, nothing physical besides kissing.

They'd simply fallen asleep together, next to each other, listening to the sound of the other breathing.

Ella had often thought that she'd know the person she was meant to be with if she enjoyed their presence just at the sound of them breathing.

And now, she found it was true.

Just listening to him in the background, even the twitch of movement as he adjusted the covers in his sleep or as he rolled one way then the other.

She smiled, her gaze shooting back to him.

The same excitement she'd felt last night prickled across her chest once more, and her smile widened. But then she glanced back at the images on her computer, and her frown returned.

"What is it?"

She looked up again.

Brenner's eyes had fluttered open, and he was stifling a yawn as he glanced in her direction.

"I think I found something," she replied.

"What time is it?"

"Early," she said.

He glanced at the red digital numbers on the clock by the bed. Then issued a small snort. It was nearly five AM.

"How long you been up?" he called.

"Only an hour... Ish," she said, wincing sheepishly.

"They teach all you federal types to work around the clock?"

She smiled sweetly back at him. "I was enjoying the view."

"Can't help but notice your back is to the window."

"Wasn't talking about the view outside."

He snorted and reached up, scratching at the scar under his chin. But she detected a small smile he was attempting to conceal.

She nodded over her shoulder towards the small kitchenette that had come with the hotel room. "Coffee."

"You're an angel."

Now it was her turn to chuckle, and again, the sound vanished as she returned her attention to the computer screen.

Brenner, picking up on this, was also frowning now. He pushed out of the bed, his muscled arms corded under the thin fabric of his white T-shirt.

He approached her, running a hand through his hair, limping off his injured leg. The cut of his T-shirt caused the neck to go low, and she glimpsed the edge of an angry, roping scar.

She stared at it, shivering.

Where they'd operated to remove the bullets he'd taken.

She reached out, holding his hand as he approached, and the two of them glanced at the screen together. She felt his hand tense in hers as he stared at the grisly images.

"What the hell? Crime scene photos?"

"No," she said. "Someone else took these. Before the coroner showed up."

Brenner leaned in, scowling now. His handsome features twisted into an expression of extreme disapproval.

The images were of the crime scenes, including the one they'd just visited at the icefields.

All of them displayed the picture-perfect features of the gorgeous women who'd fallen prey to the depravity of this most recent killer.

And each one was illuminated by the Northern Lights.

In the pictures, the victims didn't look dead but, rather, as if they were sleeping.

The pictures were high-quality, framed in such a way as to capture the beautiful landscapes behind them.

"What's this?" Brenner said quietly.

She glanced down at the caption beneath each of the victims. The first victim had a *V* under her portrait. The second had an *A*. The third had the letter *I*. Then the fourth displayed the letter *N*.

"Vain," said Brenner under his breath.

"Yeah..." Ella stared, feeling a shiver up her spine. She wasn't sure when it had happened, but she and Brenner were no longer holding hands, as she'd put both of hers on the keyboard and mouse and was now furiously scrolling down the webpage.

"Where is this site?"

"I found it through an image search," she said. "It's hosted privately."

"Does it say anything in the *About* section?"

She glanced at the top of the masthead and clicked. It opened a blank page. "Nothing."

"What's the website called."

Sevendeadly. They both read the name in silence.

"Seven deadly?"

"Yeah," she said. "As in the seven deadly sins, is my guess. Vainglory. Or Vanity is one of them."

He stared at her. And then, suddenly, he exclaimed as if he'd been stung.

She glanced sharply up and over at him. "What?" she said urgently.

But he was tapping his finger against the screen now.

And she realized what he was indicating.

There were three words on the masthead besides the empty *About* section. One said *Vainglory*. One said *Gluttony*. One said *Lust*.

With a shaking hand, Ella moved away from the framed pictures of the dead women and instead clicked on the next heading. Gluttony.

The page opened up, and she could feel her heart racing. Suddenly, she went still.

Both Brenner and she inhaled sharply, simultaneously.

More pictures. These with the letters G, L, U... onwards, under them. Spelling out Gluttony.

But these weren't victims she recognized. Instead of the beautiful, perfectly symmetrical features of their recent victims, these figures were larger. Overweight and very much unclothed, as if someone were intent on humiliating the figures in the photos.

"Dear God," Brenner whispered under his breath.

Ella wasn't sure God had participated at *all* in whatever sick, demonic mind had come up with these pictures.

"They're dead," Brenner said.

"Looks like it. Not the icefields, though. Where is this?"

"Alleyways. See the dumpsters, there? Trash cans... big ones. Like the type behind restaurants."

"He posed them behind restaurants?"

"Yeah. Posed the female victims under the Northern Lights."

Ella and Brenner both went quiet, staring at the images as she clicked through the horrible spectacles of the undressed, overweight victims left in alleys like trash.

"He's spelling out the letters to the deadly sins," she whispered. "Which means..."

Brenner tapped his finger against the final heading. *Lust.*

She didn't want to but knew she had to. So she clicked.

These photos looked older as if taken from a worse camera. Perhaps a phone from a few years before. The victims here were clothed in jackets, sweaters, thick outfits.

"He's concealing them," Brenner said. "Hang on, wait. I know this one!"

Ella stopped on a picture of a young woman who was lying dead on the side of a road.

"You do?"

"I remember this case. She was an ex-con. Was working as a prostitute."

Brenner spoke slowly, frowning as he did, as if the words brought him pain.

"She was found with her throat slit. The killer left her there like she was nothing. No identification, no leads. It went cold."

Ella felt her stomach turn as she looked at the picture of the young woman, her lifeless eyes turned towards the camera.

"The other victims," Ella said. "Why didn't I hear about this? No one mentioned it?"

"Look up the Gluttony victims. See if there were any reports."

Ella was already cycling to the encrypted FBI database, entering keyword information to scan local and federal reports for similar crimes.

The results appeared nearly instantly.

She scrolled through the reports, her eyes widening as she read the details of the cases.

"The Gluttony victims," she said, her voice shaking. "They were homeless. No one cared about them."

Brenner nodded grimly. "He's choosing victims who won't be missed. Who won't be mourned."

Ella felt sick to her stomach as she looked at the images of the victims. The killer had taken great care to capture their final moments, to make sure they were displayed in a way that was both grotesque and demeaning.

"He's a sicko," Brenner said, his voice low. "But the women... He changed his pattern. Homeless, prostitutes... He moved on to models. That's why you were called in."

Ella was shaking her head, biting her lip as she scanned through the relevant files. "He was killing one a month. Different locations in Alaska. Not just Juneau. No one connected the cases. No one even cared."

"Not until a pretty woman was involved," said Brenner, frowning. Then, he cleared his throat, coughing delicately. "Not that... er, not that I'm saying it's bad to be a pretty woman." He shot her a sidelong glance.

Ella would've smiled if she wasn't so disturbed by the images. Instead, she reached out and patted him on the arm.

This seemed to set him more at ease.

Ella tried to ignore the fear that was creeping up inside of her. She knew they were getting closer to the killer, but she couldn't shake the feeling that he was watching them, that he was always one step ahead.

"We need to find out who's behind this website," she said. "We need to trace the IP address, find out who's uploading these photos."

"Think we'll be able to?"

"Probably. But there are seven deadly sins. He's only just getting started."

"And look there."

She did. Brenner was pointing at the first heading. *"Vainglory,"* she read. And then she realized what he was saying.

Not *vain*. Vainglory... "Five more victims," she said, her breath caught in her throat. "He's going to kill five more in this category."

"And then who knows when he'll start again," Brenner replied. "Those Lust victims were from years ago."

"Same with the Gluttony ones," she said, biting her lip at the sentence, as even uttering it felt troubling.

"So once he finishes his spree, he'll disappear again," Brenner said.

Ella was now moving to her feet, pulling her phone from her pocket. "Just means we better make sure it doesn't happen."

Chapter 10

He watched her dance, swaying with the pulsing music. The scent of body sweat lingered on the air, and his eyes darted furtively around the figures on the dance floor, under the disco ball as music pumped through the club.

He twisted and fidgeted uncomfortably, unable to sit still for too long.

He'd never been very good at staying *still*. Never been good at anything really. Just a waste of time and space and air and...

He cut off this chain of thought. The cycle of berating he'd so often endured. He gripped the edge of the glass cup, squeezing until he heard a satisfying *crack*.

The glass shattered in his hand. Then the pain.

The lances of glass jutted into his palm and drew crimson beads that trickled along his fingers. He allowed himself a small smile as the blood spilled down his hand.

The pain helped him relax.

"You good, brah?" said one of the bartenders, who'd come over to clear off a table covered in pretzel dust.

The man had dreadlocks and an earnest smile. But was his gaze lingering too long? *Lust*? No... no, the man was glancing at the blood on the table. He was also moving slow. *Sloth.*

So slow.

"What's your name, brah?" said the bartender again, using the familiar truncation a second time.

"I have no name," he replied, wiping his bloody hand on a napkin, and issuing a sniff.

"No name?" asked the bartender, wrinkling his nose. "Strange that, nah?"

Brah. Brah. Nah.

No-Name shook his head in frustration. "Strange," he replied. "Please, leave me alone."

"Alright, then. Your hand, though. You bleedin'."

No-Name glanced down, sighed, looked up again, and flashed a smile. He looked once more towards the dance floor where she was swaying.

She knew she was beautiful. She wore clothing to emphasize it, arousing one of the other sins in the men and some women who watched so closely.

No-Name could feel his temper rising. He rose to his feet suddenly, pushing away from the table, and moving quickly forward.

He knew what had to be done.

Chapter 11

Ella tapped her fingers against the dashboard where the two of them sat in the parking lot, staring at the computer screen between them.

Brenner was shaking his head in frustration.

"No trace on the IP?" she said, reading his expression.

"There is, but it's not from a personal computer."

She leaned in, studying the screen, reading the reported results. Her eyes widened. "The police precinct?"

"Yeah."

The two of them looked up, staring through the window. Why was the trace on the computer that had posted those horrible pictures of the dead victims leading them back to the precinct?

Sitting in the parking lot, behind the building, Ella had expected to drive out onto the highway.

But now...

She frowned, reached out, and tentatively pushed open the door. Then, her eyes widened. "Evidence room," she whispered.

Brenner glanced at her, nodded quickly, and the two of them pushed out of the door, moving hastily towards the front of the building.

As they approached the entrance, Ella's heart was pounding in her chest. She had been in and out of this precinct countless times, but now, the thought of what they might find inside made her feel like an intruder.

Brenner held the door open for her, and they both stepped inside. The precinct was bustling with activity; officers were moving back and forth, phones ringing, and radios blaring.

Ella could feel the weight of their stares on her as she walked through the station. She had to remind herself that they were on the right side of the law.

Why was the IP address traced back here? The question reverberated in her mind.

They made their way to the evidence room and found it guarded by a large man behind a large desk.

The man was balding, and his ample hips drooped over the side of his wooden chair. The chair creaked as he leaned back, folding his hands over his belly.

"Can I help you two? Feds, right?" he said.

Ella nodded, flashing her badge. She paused, then said, "We need access to your computer, please."

He blinked, staring at her. He frowned. "Not sure I can do that."

"It's somewhat time sensitive," she said insistently.

Ella scanned the room, looking for any clues. She spotted a desk pushed against the wall with a computer on it. "Can we check the evidence room entries from that?"

He sighed, glanced past them, looked at Brenner, and frowned. But then he looked at Ella again, and his expression softened. There were *some* advantages to having a pretty face.

"Fine, fine," he muttered. "No law against checking the log." He hesitated then finally nodded. "Alright, follow me," he said, standing up from his chair and gesturing for them to follow. Instead of leading them to the computer she'd spotted, though, he moved past it, muttering, "Not connected to the network," he said. "IT still working on it. This will give you the full database."

Ella and Brenner followed the man to a door at the end of the hallway. He swiped his badge and opened the door, revealing a small room filled with computer equipment.

"Here you go," he said, pointing to a computer in the corner. "But you're not allowed to touch anything else in here."

Brenner walked over to the computer and started typing away. "I'm going to run a search," he said.

Ella's eyes darted around the room, taking in the shelves of evidence bags and boxes.

Brenner murmured, "Only three laptops in the evidence room."

"What about this computer?" she asked quietly.

He shook his head. "No IP match. But check the third shelf. Log number 25J."

Ella nodded quickly, following the directive.

She walked over to the third shelf and pulled out the evidence bag labeled "25J." She could feel her heart pounding in her chest as she unzipped the bag and pulled out the laptop.

It was small and unassuming, with no visible markings or stickers. But as she opened it up and turned it on, she paused in surprise. "Battery life," she muttered slowly. She frowned.

The screen lit up to reveal a login prompt. She paused, biting her lower lip. Then attempted a password: *Lust.*

Nothing.

Gluttony.

Nothing.

Vainglory.

The computer screen changed, revealing a desktop with a blank, black background.

"I'm in," she said, her voice shaky. "It's his. It's the killer's laptop."

"Are you sure?"

"Yeah. Vainglory was the password."

"Shit. What's the killer's laptop doing in an evidence lockup?"

Ella shivered briefly, shaking her head. She was staring at the only file on the computer.

A folder in the center of the desktop. It was labeled "Artwork."

Her hand shook slightly as she clicked on the folder, revealing dozens of images and videos as thumbnails. She didn't need to look long to realize they were pictures of the victims.

"It's his. They're all here. All except for Laura."

"The most recent victim?"

Ella nodded.

Ella stared at the images of the deceased victims. There was such an eerie, grotesque beauty to it all. It made her skin prickle. She couldn't stare at it and glanced away.

But she couldn't look away for long. They needed to find out who was responsible for this.

As she continued scrolling through the images, she noticed a file labeled "INSTRUCTIONS." She clicked on it and a document opened up.

It was a step-by-step guide on how to pose the bodies, complete with detailed instructions on how to dispose of the victims and avoid detection. As if the killer had been writing a how-to manual on grisly photoshoots.

Ella felt a cold chill run down her spine as she read through the document. It was clear that whoever had written it had hoped to disseminate their work.

"What case is this?" she said, turning back to Brenner.

He was already looking at the computer screen, frowning. "Looks like a hit and run. A few days ago. Laptop was found in the back of the trunk."

"A hit and run?"

"Mhmm. No witnesses."

"What about the victim?"

"No victim. The killer apparently drove his car off the road into a parked snowmobile. Probably distracted going through his murder photos."

Ella wrinkled her nose. She looked back at the laptop. "And they couldn't trace whose this was?"

"No. No ID. No email connected. The killer didn't access the internet from this."

"Have we checked with the manufacturer about the serial number?"

"Yeah."

Brenner paused.

"What is it?"

He was frowning now, scratching at his chin. "Huh," he said.

"What?"

"Funny thing..." He looked at her, eyebrows rising. "The computer was owned by a small business where Jeremy Watkins works."

"Jeremy..." she trailed off, her eyes rising. "Our latest victim's boyfriend? He likes riding snowmobiles, doesn't he?"

"Yeah. At least that's what he mentioned in his interview."

"So this laptop was owned by Jeremy?"

"No. He owns a coffee shop, and the laptop was owned by the shop. But under his purview."

"We need to speak with Laura's boyfriend."

Brenner was nodding.

Ella scanned the computer once more, making sure the bare face of it didn't conceal anything beneath. Then, shaking her head, she took the computer with her.

Perhaps it was a longshot, but maybe someone in IT could find something that had been missed.

She followed Brenner out of the room, frowning. She felt troubled now, marching hurriedly out the evidence room door.

Chapter 12

Jeremy Watkins was leaning against the one-way window in the back of the interrogation room, having refused a seat.

Ella faced him, having seated herself across the table.

Brenner was watching the two of them from his position by the door.

Jeremy looked nervous, twitchy. He had long, shoulder-length hair. A portion of it was pulled back with a red scrunchie, but most of it just hung loose. His ears were pierced in multiple places, and he had a nose ring.

His features were sharp, almost feminine, but distinctly handsome. He had a smile that was more camouflage than warmth, and his arms crossed defensively over his chest where he reclined.

"Why don't you take a seat," Brenner said, nodding at the chair across the table.

"You said this wasn't an arrest."

"No, but you'll get tired just standing. This might take a while."

"Nah. I'm good."

Brenner frowned.

Ella leaned forward, steepling her hands under her chin. "I was hoping we could ask you about this."

She slid a laptop across the table.

It wasn't the laptop from the evidence room. But it looked identical. The one with the killer's photos on it was currently with IT, being picked apart.

This one, though, had been loaned by one of the beat cops. It had no markings, no decals.

Ella slid it confidently across the table, though. As she did, she watched Jeremy's expression.

He didn't move. Didn't blink.

If anything, he just stood there, frozen in place. Like most of the icefields.

"What's that?" he said.

"A laptop."

"I know that. I mean why are you showing it to me?"

He seemed hesitant, uncertain. But there was no flicker of recognition in his eyes. Then again, Ella knew sociopaths were often masters at hiding their emotions.

"You don't know?" she said.

He gave a quick, jolting shake of his head, causing long locks of hair to shift across his face.

Ella slowly stood now, facing him across the table.

She moved around the table now, sitting on the edge closest to him, effectively cutting off the emotional barrier provided by the table. One of the courses she'd taken and excelled in, among many, back in school had been human psychology and body language.

Now, she watched as Jeremy fidgeted uncomfortably, arms wrapped around himself.

"This computer is registered to your business."

"What?"

She didn't repeat the comment, preferring to allow the uncomfortable silence to fill the space between them.

He hesitated, stammered. "I... I don't know anything about that."

"And yet it's the truth," she said quietly. "And do you know what we found on the computer?"

"Why would I know! I thought this was about Laura. You told me this was about her death!"

Brenner cut in now, his voice gruff, "You don't sound too broken up about it."

Jeremy whirled on Brenner now. The effeminate, handsome features twisted into something of a snarl. "You don't know me, man." His nose bunched up, taking the nose ring with it, and causing the fake diamond to flash under the bright light above. "I'm grieving in my own way."

"Sure you are," Brenner said, communicating with his tone the opposite belief.

Jeremy was shaking his head now, staring at the computer, his eyes the size of saucers, his gaze fixated. "What... what's on it?"

Ella paused, still watching him. She then crossed her arms, leaning back. "Pictures of the deceased. There were more victims than we first imagined."

"How many more?" he said reflexively. He swallowed, his Adam's apple bobbing.

"More," she said simply. "Where were you when Laura was attacked?"

"I... I told you. At home."

"You said you dropped her off."

"Yeah! Yeah, but then I went home."

"How do you know you were home the exact time she was attacked?" Ella said. She knew this wasn't a very fair question, but she was hoping to catch him in a lie.

He stared at her, mouth unhinged. "What the hell is this? I'm guessing. I thought you wanted me to help you find the guy... You don't think... don't think *I* had anything to do with it, do you?"

His voice was shrill now, and his hands had bunched at his sides.

Ella didn't reply. His earnest tone was pleading for some sort of placation, to calm him. But she wasn't willing to give it. Not yet. Not now.

The stakes were too high.

Vainglory.

More victims on the horizon. The killer was still out there, on the hunt.

Who knew when he'd strike again. And if they didn't catch him in time, he'd disappear, returning later. The same way he'd done with the *lust* killings. The *gluttony* killings.

She frowned, hesitating briefly, tracing the palm of her hand with her thumb. For a moment, she wondered at the seven deadly sins.

She looked at where Jeremy was shaking his head, and then she murmured, "Do you know anything about the seven sins?"

"Wh-what?" he looked completely discombobulated now.

"The seven deadly sins," she said softly. "Do you know anything about them?"

"No! What? Why would I?"

"Take a moment and think before you answer," Brenner growled.

Jeremy shot an uncomfortable look at the lanky lawman and seemed to shrivel in on himself, his shoulders hunching.

He let out a long sigh, closed his eyes, and then murmured, "I mean... sure. I guess I've heard of them."

"Can you list them for me?" Ella said.

"No."

"Try," Brenner snapped.

"What is this, man?"

"Just try, please," Ella said, her tone more calm but still firm.

He rolled his eyes, looking very much like a petulant child caught with his hand in a cookie jar. But then, he let out a long sigh, and, after glancing at the two of them briefly, he muttered. "I mean... whatever, man. One was... death... No, wait... Umm... Pride, right?"

Ella didn't reply.

He continued, "And there's... greed, and... uh... sloth, and... wrath?" He looked at them for confirmation.

Ella nodded her head slowly, silently urging him to continue.

"Envy?" he said, more like a question than a statement.

"Two more," Brenner said, his voice gruff.

"I don't know! I don't know!" Jeremy exclaimed, throwing his hands up in the air.

Ella leaned forward, her eyes locked on his. "Lust and gluttony."

Jeremy's eyes widened, and he licked his lips nervously. "Right, right," he murmured. "Why do you ask?" he said, his voice shaking.

"Just curious," Ella said with a shrug. "But let me ask you something else. Do you think any of these sins apply to you?"

"What? No! I mean... what kind of question is that?"

"Just answer the question, Jeremy," Brenner growled.

Jeremy hesitated, his eyes darting between Ella and Brenner. "I don't know," he finally said. "I mean, I'm not perfect. I've made mistakes. But who hasn't?"

"That's not an answer," Ella said. "Do you think you've committed any of these sins?"

"I... I don't know," he said, his voice barely above a whisper.

Ella leaned back in her chair, studying him. She could see the fear in his eyes, the uncertainty. But she couldn't tell if it was because he was guilty or just scared of this line of questioning.

She said, "What about wrath? Do you ever find yourself so angry, you just need to lash out?"

"No! No, it's not like that."

He was leaning back now as if trying to get the wall behind him to swallow him.

He was shaking his head adamantly, clearly nervous and uncomfortable.

Ella lowered her hands where she'd crossed them. She was watching him, but now starting to wonder if she'd made a mistake.

The laptop was traced back to his place of business, though. So she said, "Do you have laptops at your establishment?"

"Wh-what... Umm, yeah. Yeah, we do. But we have a bunch."

"Have any gone missing recently?"

"We sometimes replace them. When they get old. I mean, if that's one of 'em, it's like five years old. A dinosaur as far as tech goes."

"You know tech?" Brenner asked.

"I mean, some. Yeah."

"You like new things, don't you?" Brenner asked. "Beautiful things. But the things you find beautiful aren't what others might agree with, are they? Do you fancy yourself an amateur photographer? Do you know anything about cameras?"

Jeremy endured this line of questioning while wincing. He hesitated, shaking his head after each comment. "I... What?" He looked back at Ella as if searching for help.

She didn't reply at first. But the look of confusion on his face seemed genuine, so she said, "Is there any way a laptop went missing from your establishment?"

"Umm... Possibly. If we dumped them, someone could've snatched it. I dunno. The laptops are used by customers, too. It's part of our business model to attract itinerants." He looked at Brenner. "Itinerant means someone who's come from one place to another."

Brenner glared at the veiled jab.

Ella, though, was becoming more uncertain the more they spoke with the man.

She couldn't be sure if he was telling the truth or not. But if the laptops were available publicly, then there was a chance the killer had stumbled upon them. Maybe that's how he had found Laura, through Jeremy's shop.

Or maybe Jeremy was an accomplished liar.

"Wait!" Jeremy said suddenly. He was grinning now. "Wait, wait! Let me show you!"

"Show us what?" Ella asked.

"I have proof I couldn't have hurt Laura. Right after I left her! I was live-streaming on my snowmobile. Like *right* after!"

Ella paused. The scene of the crime had been a complicated, convoluted thing. It would've taken time for the killer to set it all up.

"Can you show us the footage?" she asked.

"Of course, of course!" Jeremy said, his face brightening. "I'll show you right now!"

He moved quickly towards the small side table with a gray tupperware where he'd placed his personal effects on entry at Brenner's request. As he moved, he almost knocked over a chair in the process; he bounded over to the small desk against the wall. He fished his phone, his hand trembling in equal parts discomfort and apparent excitement.

"Here, here!" he said, gesturing for them to come closer. "Just let me pull up the file."

Ella and Brenner exchanged a glance and then slowly walked over. They stood behind Jeremy, watching as he clicked through folders, muttering to himself.

"Got it!" he said, a moment later. "Here!"

He hit play, and the screen flickered to life.

Ella leaned in, watching as the video loaded. She could see Jeremy, bundled up in thick clothes, helmet on his head, revving up a snowmobile. He was grinning, waving at the camera. She checked the timestamp. Twenty minutes before the coroner's estimated time of death.

"Here we go! You knuckleheads think you can keep up with *me*? Fat chance, Eli!" Jeremy shouted in the video. And then he was off, tearing through the snow, the camera jostling wildly.

Ella watched, her heart sinking. The video was almost ten minutes long. Heading *away* from the crime scene.

But then, towards the end of the clip, something caught her eye.

It was a flash of movement, just out of the corner of the screen.

She reached out, paused the video. "What was that?"

Jeremy turned around, looking confused. "What?"

"Go back. Let me see that again, please."

Jeremy rewound the video, and Ella focused on the spot where she had seen the movement. As the snowmobile roared through the snow, she saw a figure darting across the screen, disappearing behind a thick grove of trees as if attempting to hide.

"Stop!" she said, and Jeremy paused the video again. "Can you zoom in?"

He fiddled with the controls, and the image on the screen grew larger. Ella leaned in, studying the figure. It was too small to make out any features, but she could see that it was a person, running away from the snowmobile.

"Who's that?" Brenner said, leaning in to get a better look.

"I don't know," Jeremy said, shaking his head. "I didn't see anyone."

Ella's mind was racing. She studied the figure on the screen, trying to commit every detail to memory.

"Can you enhance the image?" she asked, glancing at Jeremy.

"I don't know if I can," he said, looking hesitant. "I'm not really an expert on this stuff."

Brenner leaned in instead, clicking a tab that read *Sharpness Filtration.*

He fiddled with the controls, and the image on the screen grew even larger, the pixels blurring as he zoomed in.

Ella leaned in closer, her heart racing. The figure was still too small to make out any features, but she could see that it was a man wearing dark clothing.

"Can you print this?" she asked, turning to Brenner. "I want to take it back..."

As he began to nod, a loud knocking suddenly reverberated against the door.

Jeremy jumped, yelping in surprise.

Brenner and Ella both turned.

The door swung open, and a man was standing there, his face pale, his eyes wide. He was breathing heavily, having clearly just run down the hall.

"What is it?" Brenner asked.

The man's nostrils flared, and then he said, his voice shaking, "We... we have a situation."

"What is it?" Brenner repeated a bit more emphatically.

The cop in the door paused, shooting an uncomfortable look at Jeremy, who was pretending to look away as if he wasn't listening.

But then, the cop shrugged. He cleared his throat, took a long breath after a deep swallow, and said, "We have another murder. They just found the body. It's still on scene."

Brenner stood stunned.

Ella felt her heart plummet. Jeremy's alibi was solid, but not nearly as solid as *this*. He was being interrogated during another murder.

Back to square one.

More than that, another soul snuffed from the earth.

She scowled, brushing past the cop in the door and moving hurriedly into the dark hallway that led to the exit.

"Text me the coordinates, please!" she called over her shoulder.

"We leaving right now?" Brenner called back.

In answer, Ella curtly nodded her head a single time, picking up her pace.

Chapter 13

Ella shivered, staring at where the body hung suspended over the icefields.

She watched as Brenner twisted at a piece of wire wrapped around the woman's ankle. He grunted as he tried to pry the barb loose, helping one of the forensic techs extricate the metal from the soft, cold skin.

Her stomach felt spoiled, and her heart panged in her chest.

The icefields glistened off to the side.

The sun streaked the surface, resplendent hues painted across the ice. The body was wrapped in a leather jacket and thick, black boots encased the woman's feet.

Ella leaned in, staring at the boots. There were scuffs on the bottom, mud-caking between the rubber cracks. The boots were large... too large.

She frowned.

"What is it?" Brenner said, breathing heavily from the exertion of helping to cut the body down. His words were nearly lost by the cacophony of other voices behind them, near the emergency vehicles.

Ella shook her head, exhaustion beginning to weigh on her. The afternoon sun beat down around them, illuminating the cold ground.

"The shoes," Ella said softly, moving closer so Brenner could hear her over the sound of an arguing coroner and police officer. They sounded as if they were debating chain of custody for the evidence.

"What about them?"

"Wrong size."

Brenner leaned in. "You sure?"

"Yeah. Also... look at her. Makeup-streaked features. A face like that?"

"She was probably once stunning."

"Yeah. So why is she wearing work boots caked in mud?"

"Dunno. Hobby? Pastime?"

"Or... they're not her boots."

Brenner nodded slowly, scratching at the side of his face. Now, a cart was being wheeled over by two paramedics. The body was finally able to be lowered.

Ella looked away, unwilling to watch.

"Coroner suggested time of death was hours ago, maybe longer," Brenner said.

"Yeah. I heard."

"So this guy might be out there already killing again."

"He's escalating. Moving faster. Think he knows we found his laptop?"

"Maybe. Still feel as if we should be able to trace the owner of it."

"We did. But the owner is innocent."

Brenner shook his head, glancing at the mud-caked boots again. "So you think the boots belong to the killer?"

"It's possible..." She tapped a finger against her lips.

"What is it?"

"I was wondering if maybe we can trace the mud."

"The mud? Like finding where it's from."

"Soil sample, yeah. How hard do you think that would be?"

"I can ask someone. Give me a sec."

Brenner turned, moving quickly towards the forensic tech he'd been helping earlier.

Ella watched as the two men spoke in quick, rushed voices. Brenner was gesturing at his shoes, then over to Ella again.

She couldn't hear what they were saying, but she could see the urgency in their movements. The sun continued to beat down on her, but Ella barely noticed. Her mind was whirring with possibilities. If they could trace the mud, they might be able to find the killer's hideout.

Brenner jogged back over to her, a grim expression on his face. "They're willing to try. They need to take a soil sample from the boots, and then they'll compare it to samples from the surrounding area. If they rush it, accuracy might be compromised, but it's still doable."

Ella nodded. "Good. Let's do it."

They stood by silently as the techs took the sample. Ella couldn't help but glance at the body again. The woman's lifeless face seemed to be staring straight at her. It was a haunting image.

Finally, the soil sample was taken, and the techs rushed off, having bagged the particles. Ella and Brenner watched as they disappeared into one of the emergency vehicles.

"What do you think our killer is doing right now?" Brenner asked suddenly, breaking the silence.

Ella shrugged. "Maybe he's watching us. Maybe he's planning his next move."

"I just..." Brenner frowned. "I can't shake the emblem."

"The skull?"

"Yeah. If our killer is a SEAL member and if he's the one who popped our tires, he might still be watching us."

"Can you think of a way to lure him out?" she said.

Brenner considered this for a moment, frowning as he did. "We were trained to blend in. Usually, if you notice a SEAL, it's too late."

"There's got to be *something* we can do to lure him out..."

"Well..." Brenner paused. "Someone ambushed the road at the airfield. Maybe if we let it leak that some big-wig investigators are coming in to help... He might want to slow them too."

"Let it leak how?"

"APB on unsecured channels."

Ella paused, considering this. She tried to put the pieces together. The flower skull of a SEAL team Brenner knew. The ambushed road from the airfield. The photos on the laptop. The posed bodies.

Something connected it all... but she didn't know *what*.

Finally, she glanced at Brenner and said, "Let's do it. See if we can bait him out. Ambush the ambusher."

"On it," Brenner said, reaching for his walkie-talkie.

Chapter 14

No-Name sat in the back of his camper van, listening to the radio static.

His eyes narrowed, and he stood to his feet.

"Investigators coming in... can you pick them up, Adams?"

No-Name scowled, his teeth worrying at his lip as he paced back and forth inside his off-grid means of transportation. He leaned forward, peering out the window at the trees beyond, the slopes of the mountains in the distance, standing sentry against the horizon.

A faint gust of cold wind ushered through a crack under the window, causing him to shiver. Then scowl.

He continued his pacing, muttering under his breath now, shaking his head hurriedly side to side.

More investigators. They needed *more.* Because he was just too smart for them.

"No!" he said suddenly, snarling. "NO! Arrogance. I'm not smart. I'm a weasel! Stupid! Stupid!" He banged his head against the side of the camper van, grimacing in pain, but refusing to make a sound.

Weakness merited *more* punishment.

His head throbbed in pain, and he reached out with tremoring fingers—one hand bandaged from where glass had gouged earlier—and turned up the volume on the radio.

A crackling sound of static gave way to the words, *"Time is moved up. Twenty minutes after the hour. Investigators think they have a lead..."*

He listened pensively, frowning as he did, rubbing his fingers against the tattoo of a skull made of floral patterns on his wrist.

A tattoo from a different life. From his past.

He shivered briefly, standing there, listening.

And then he nodded to himself. Snatched keys off the hook on the wall and shoved out the door.

He paused only long enough to fish his hand back in and snatch the long rifle with the scope leaning against the aluminum interior.

And then he moved quickly, hastening towards his parked ATV.

They hadn't gotten the message the first time.

This time, he wouldn't be nearly so restrained.

Chapter 15

Ella and Brenner sat in their SUV, hidden on the side of the road, both of them watching the path leading from the airport.

Around them, two other vehicles were also pulled over, also concealed under the shadows of the foliage.

Ella could hear Brenner breathing heavily.

Both of them were tense. Her hands gripped each other if only to give herself something sturdy to cling to in that moment.

The lights were off. The engines off.

All of them were watching the trees, watching the road.

"Are we sure there are only two trails leading here?" Ella whispered.

Brenner nodded, jamming a thumb over his shoulder to indicate the vehicle behind them. "That's what Ant said."

Ella glanced back at the police sergeant sitting in the vehicle behind them. Ant Lehman was an older man, with a paunch and an impressive gray beard.

He wasn't exactly her first choice for backup.

But at least they had backup. Two police per squad car. And the two of them.

Six against one.

Ella shivered again, squeezing her hands once more.

"Here they come," Brenner said quietly.

The two of them glanced towards the vehicle trundling down the path, coming from the direction of the airfield.

"Bullet-proof glass, right?" Ella said.

Brenner gave a quick nod.

This put her a bit more at ease. She didn't like the idea of leading anyone into an ambush. But now her anticipation mounted as she watched the sleek sedan with the tinted windows moving slowly towards them. Behind them, Ella thought she spotted an airplane picking off the airfield and heading south once again.

Her heart pounded in her chest. Her breath caught.

The tension seemed to mount in the form of her held breath and Brenner's nervous tapping of his foot against the ground.

"Think he'll come?" Brenner whispered.

"Don't know," Ella replied.

The two of them stared through the windshield, keeping track of the trails, ears and eyes peeled.

As the sedan drew closer, Ella could feel her heart pounding in her chest, her hands slick with sweat. She tried to steady her breathing, tried to calm herself down, but it was no use. This was it. They were about to find out if they were right. If the killer would come.

The sedan slowed to a stop in front of their vehicle, the tinted windows hiding the man inside. Ella could feel her nerves fraying at the edges, her mind racing through all the possible outcomes of this encounter.

Finally, the window rolled down, revealing a man sitting behind the wheel. He was middle-aged, with thinning hair and sharp features, his eyes scanning the area around them with a practiced ease.

"Detectives," he said smoothly, inclining his head in greeting.

Ella nodded back.

"I was told my job was just to... linger," the middle-aged man said.

Brenner nodded. "Keep the windows up," he added. "Stay inside the car."

Brenner kept glancing off in the direction of the mountains as if searching for *something*.

Ella was frowning into the car, though.

The middle-aged man wasn't smiling. What she'd initially taken for practiced ease, she realized, was a cavalier indifference.

No... no, perhaps not *cavalier.*

Indifference, though. As if he didn't expect to find anything outside the car.

His brow prickled with sweat. And she watched closely as he swallowed, his Adam's apple bobbing.

He looked nervous. Uncomfortable and scared.

"Is everything alright, sir?" she said cautiously.

Brenner looked sharply over at her tone, clearly detecting something in her voice.

The man was still trying to force a smile and an easy-going expression, but now that Ella was looking, she could see through it.

Her eyes trailed along his face, moving towards the woods again then back at him.

"What's wrong, sir?" she repeated, a bit more firmly.

He cleared his throat, hesitated, then gave a nervous little chuckle. "Er... what do you mean? Everything's fine."

He was trying, but not very hard. His heart wasn't in this comment. She didn't believe him for a second.

She noticed now what he was doing with his eyes. Slowly moving them as if glancing back over his shoulder.

Into the backseat.

And suddenly a thought struck her. Ice filled her veins, and her heart hammered.

She turned, ever so slightly, glancing into the backseat.

And that's when she spotted him.

There, in the dark, concealed in the shadows provided by upholstery and leather a figure was crouched behind the front seat.

A figure with a gun in hand pointed directly at the middle-aged cop.

The figure's eyes met Ella's.

And suddenly there was a loud shout.

"DRIVE!"

The middle-aged man yelled as the gun was jammed into his ribs.

Ella reeled back as the car's tires sped against the ground, spitting dust.

Confusion reigned briefly, but Brenner reacted first, drawing his own gun with lightning-fast reflexes. But he didn't have a clear shot.

The car sprang forward, speeding past them, racing quickly up the trail.

"He's in the back seat!" Ella was shouting. "The killer is in the back!"

How had that happened? When had he slipped in?

If anything, this confirmed Brenner's theory that they were dealing with more than their usual run-of-the-mill psychopath.

Now, the two of them were sprinting back towards their own car. The other police vehicles were moving off the side of the road, driving in hot pursuit.

The three law enforcement vehicles created a thin tail behind the speeding, bullet-proof sedan ahead of them.

Ella didn't buckle, desperately rolling down her window and allowing the wind to whip through the cabin as Brenner took the wheel, speeding after the fleeing car.

The chase was on. The sedan ahead of them was driving recklessly, swerving through the narrow mountain road. Brenner skillfully maneuvered their car, keeping pace with the vehicle while avoiding the hazardous cracks in the asphalt edges along the way.

Ella had her gun at the ready, her eyes locked on the car's backseat. The killer was still there, but he was out of sight.

Suddenly, the sedan made a sharp turn down a dirt path which, judging by the structure in the distance, led to a small cabin. Brenner followed suit, their car kicking up dirt as they sped down the path.

The other police vehicles were close behind them, sirens blaring.

The car disappeared for a second, and there was a skidding sound.

Ella and Brenner moved around the switchback, coming in sight of the cabin, and then Brenner hit the brakes.

They were both breathing heavily, staring at the cabin.

The sedan was parked up against the steps, the doors flung open.

No sign of movement.

Brenner addressed her but kept his eyes on the cabin. "He meant to bring us here," Brenner whispered.

"Think it's a trap?"

"I know it is," he replied.

As they approached the cabin, Ella could see movement in the trees as the two cop cars joined them on the trail. She signaled to Brenner, and they both exited the car, guns drawn.

They slowly made their way towards the cabin, their eyes scanning the area for any sign of danger.

Suddenly, shots rang out from within the cabin. Ella and Brenner quickly took cover behind nearby trees, returning fire.

The bullets whistled past them, hitting the trees and sending splinters flying. Ella could hear the other police officers shouting over the radio, calling for backup and giving their location.

But they couldn't wait for backup. They had to take down the killer before he escaped.

Brenner signaled to her, pointing to the front door of the cabin. They both nodded.

Ella could feel her chest constricting. Adrenaline pumped through her system.

More gunshots from inside the cabin.

This time, she didn't see where the bullets struck. Perhaps he was aiming at the cops who'd also exited their vehicles.

"Have to approach slowly," Brenner said urgently. "Use the trees for cover. He's a good shot."

She nodded to show she'd heard.

The two of them kept low, waited for a lull in the gunfire, then moved, breaking forth from behind the trees.

The cabin was small, with a single door and a small window to the side. The gunfire had stopped, and Ella and Brenner crept around the side of the cabin. They could hear the sound of footsteps from inside.

Brenner gestured to her, and they both squatted down, hiding behind a porch railing. Splinters rubbed against Ella's shoulder where she crouched.

She could feel her palms sweating against the grip of her gun. She took a deep breath and nodded to Brenner, who had his gun at the ready.

They both burst through the door.

The cabin was empty.

Sounds of gunfire erupted again.

And Ella ducked, but she realized a second later it was coming from the speaker of a phone left near the open window.

She stared.

"Cop's phone," Brenner guessed. "He distracted us." There was disgust in his voice.

Ella's heart sank. They had been too late.

"How?" she said. "We would've seen him leave."

She and Brenner both glanced around the small, cramped space, searching for any sign of an egress.

The windows were facing the front. The back door was shut and would've been covered by the police who'd flanked the cabin.

"Clear!" Brenner called out over his shoulder through the window. "Check the back!"

"Got it!" came a reply from outside.

Ella heard the sound of boots against detritus as the cops moved to comply with the directive.

Ella glanced around the small, cramped space, searching.

She looked past a table, glancing once more towards the backdoor. She tried to open it, but it was bolted.

From the inside.

She frowned, still moving.

And then the sound of her footsteps changed.

Sturdy taps against the floor turned to a hollow *thunk*.

She froze, frowned, stared down.

And then she saw it. A trapdoor hidden under a carpet in the corner of the room. Her heart leapt with hope. Could the killer still be here? She gestured to Brenner, pointing at the trapdoor.

Brenner nodded, his eyes narrowing as the two of them walked over to it. Brenner lifted the carpet, revealing the door. He pulled it open, and the damp scent of earth wafted up to meet their nostrils.

Brenner went first, his gun at the ready, while Ella followed closely behind. The ladder creaked as they descended into the darkness.

Ella could hear the sound of running water from below. As they descended, the sound of running water grew louder.

Ella's feet touched a mossy floor cover, and she glanced down, realizing they were standing on a small, underground stream. The water had cut through the rock, causing verdant moss to grow in clumps along the sides.

But also something else...

Her foot nudged something.

She stared down.

And then nearly stumbled back.

A skull was staring up at her. Gaping eye-sockets seemingly staring into her soul.

She stumbled back and kicked something else. More bones clattered as she realized she was standing amidst a terrain covered in bones.

Human remains.

At least six bodies she could count.

"What is this?" Brenner asked.

"A grave," she replied softly. "Maybe these were the killer's first victims."

"He's long gone," Brenner said, pointing up the tunnel, his finger following the curve of the stream.

There was no sign of the kidnapped cop or the killer. No sign of anyone.

Ella shivered, staring, her heart in her throat.

"Crap," she muttered.

"Yeah." Brenner let out a curse.

The two of them stood by the underground stream amidst the bones, both lost in their own thoughts.

Moments like these... bringing a faint lull... Ella thought it was over.

But Brenner had warned her.

The killer was leading them into a trap. She heard the gunshot.

A loud *bang*.

Distant. Echoing.

And then... as if the bullet had triggered something nearby. There came an explosion.

Chapter 16

It was as if someone had turned the world upside-down and shaken it.

Ella was thrown backward, amidst debris from the rock wall. Stones scattered as well. Voices echoed desperately.

Her back struck the ground, her head aching, her ears ringing. Someone had set off an explosion.

The tunnel had collapsed around them.

Stones now weighed heavily against her legs and her left arm.

She wasn't sure if she was upside down or right-side up.

Her back wedged against rocky protrusions.

Her head was aching. Blood was pooling down her forehead in slick, warm streams.

She groaned, grateful to find that at least her lips still worked.

"Brenner?" she tried to call out. But her voice was hoarse, faint and weak.

Pain lanced through her shoulder. She tried to sit up, but the rocks pinning her down prevented her from doing so. Her shoulder ached, but she could move her arm more. She tried to brush the blood from her face but realized she couldn't move her right arm, either.

She glanced down and realized something was wrong. She tried to wiggle her fingers and her hand to no avail. It took her a second to realize her arm wasn't broken but wedged between her ribs and the chasm wall. She couldn't move either of her legs. She also couldn't move her feet.

Her body was trapped, wedged between rocks and boulders.

"Brenner!" she shouted, and she heard her voice echo back, her voice getting raspier as she called for him.

He must be trapped with her, but in the dark, she wouldn't be able to find him.

Her shoulder was aching and she struggled to think. She moved her body as best she could, wincing as she did. No horribly jarring pain. Bruises, yes. Aches, yes. Blood, yes.

But no lances of agony from a broken spine or a broken bone.

At least not yet.

Her fingers touched something cold.

She realized her hand was in the stream. How deep was the stream?

If the water was still flowing, it meant there were still gaps.

She shivered, shifting her body a bit more, towards the water.

Rocks fell. A large section of the cavern, she realized, had collapsed across the stream, like a bridge. Which meant there was space *under* that bridge where the water was flowing.

Fear lanced through her as she managed to extricate her legs.

If she could slip under the rocks, through the stream, she might be able to escape out the other side. To find Brenner.

But if she went underwater and got trapped.

If the other side was blocked.

Horror welled within her at the thought of drowning alone in the dark.

"Brenner?" she called again.

Still no reply.

Was he unconscious?

Terror flooded through her.

Worse?

She had to move. Brenner was in danger. A killer was getting away with a hostage.

She ignored the bones around her. Making a mental note to report them when she had the chance. She exhaled deeply, and then tugged, hard, pulling an arm free. It scraped along the rocks, but her sudden motion dislodged her wrist. With no small amount of pain, she dislodged her next arm.

Then came the hard part.

She slipped over the edge of the stream-bed, delicately lowering herself into the cold water.

She hyperventilated briefly, drew breath, and then took the plunge.

Darkness around her.

Cool, silty water flowing against her body.

She grabbed the rocks and held on.

She kicked with her legs, trying to stay down, trying to go under.

Water filled her nostrils and she almost panicked.

Then she realized she was underwater, her body submerged, her head inches away from the rocks.

She kicked for the rocks.

Breathed in water.

And almost lost it.

She kicked hard. Her head broke the surface.

And then she realized she had gone off course. The rocks she had been pushing against were actually dead ahead of her.

She tried to turn around, to push herself back, but the current was strong.

She tried to swim against the current, but she was being carried forward.

Her head was above water, but she instinctively tried to move her head downward.

She felt her hair hit the rocks.

And then she gasped.

The current was carrying her into a hole.

Not a hole, a tunnel.

Rocks scraped against her head and shoulders.

She felt a bruise, a painful pressure that throbbed with every beat of her heart.

The tunnel was narrow.

She tried to use her feet to push herself along.

She could swim. The fear was a distraction. She frowned to herself, forcing the fear back. Adrenaline coursed through her. She'd been spelunking before, had dived in icy waters.

This was just another mental and physical challenge.

Her head bumped against the rocks again. She took a final breath before the section of rock that forced her to submerge and then she dove.

Underwater, no place for her head to rise, stone scraping her back, she moved through the dark, pulling herself along the silty floor.

A strange calm had descended on her. Courage from deep within. Perhaps it was the thought of Brenner, somewhere in this darkness, looking for her.

But also from an iron will.

From her refusal to allow fear to dominate her life. Courage was a choice, not a feeling.

And so she continued forward, her fingers scrabbling along the slick floor. She moved up the tunnel, her head serving to tell her when the rock dissipated.

Her lungs were aching now.

She needed to breathe, but she couldn't rise from the dark. She couldn't emerge from the water. The stone ceiling completely sealed off this option.

The cold nipped at her, swaddled her.

She kept going, her heart pounding in her chest wildly.

She had to make it.

No going back now. She was nearly out of air—she'd come too far. Turning back would simply be suicide.

She didn't know what lay ahead, but stopping wasn't an option. Retreat wasn't an option.

She'd made up her mind.

Courage wasn't a feeling. She kept reminding herself. It wasn't a feeling.

And then the stone against the back of her head disappeared suddenly.

She pushed a final time, kicking, and she found air above her.

Desperately, she gave another kick off the rocky terrain, and she emerged, her head rising out of the water.

She let out a desperate gasp, gulping greedily at the air, water pouring down her face, her arms.

She was standing in the stream, trembling, in the dark, but breathing sweet, sweet air.

"Ella?" a voice called.

She turned sharply, spotting a light glowing in the dark.

"Who is it?" she demanded, her voice startled.

"Brenner," said the whisper.

She relaxed, recognizing the lanky frame of the handsome marshal now as he approached.

He looked in much better shape than her, still limping on his bad leg, but now extending a hand to help her from the water.

She gratefully accepted his aid.

He pulled her onto dry land.

"You okay?" Brenner was whispering.

"Fine," she said. She winced as she did, testing her limbs. Nothing broken. Everything bruised.

"You?"

"I jumped clear," he said. "Spotted the TNT a second too late to warn you. Shit—sorry. You're bleeding."

"I'm fine," she said, trying to push his hand away from where it touched gently at her forehead.

The glow from Brenner's phone illuminated the dark space around them. She knew better than to try her own phone until it had ample time to dry off.

"See anything?" she whispered.

"Nothing. Tunnel leads further up that way."

There was an offer in these words. A suggestion. She hesitated, staring up the tunnel illuminated by the glow of the phone.

Brenner's arm was touching her shoulder as if he wanted to draw her close but didn't do it out of fear of offending her.

She took a wobbly step forward and nearly fell.

Brenner cursed, reaching out to catch her. He guided her gently to the ground. "Sit," he said. "You're hurt."

"I'm not," she insisted, trying to rise again.

"Just sit!" he snapped, his voice angry all of a sudden.

She scowled in the dark but then sighed, leaning back and letting out a long breath. Maybe he was right. There was no telling if the killer had rigged another trap further in.

No sense in going in half-cocked. They couldn't retreat, either. The exit through the cabin was completely blocked.

"He shot the TNT," Ella said. "I didn't even see him."

"He was in the water," Brenner replied. "I spotted him a hair late." His voice was filled with guilt as he said this.

He was crouched next to her now, studying her, fear in his eyes.

"I'm fine," she insisted. "I promise. Just a little banged up. Bruised."

"Your head."

She reached up, pulling away red-stained fingers. She shrugged. "A scrape. It barely hurts."

She reclined against the stone, though, closing her eyes briefly, allowing the exhaustion weighing on her to slowly dissipate in those passing seconds.

"How did the killer get in the car?" she whispered.

"He must've pretended to be a chauffeur," Brenner said. "Maybe even came to the precinct."

"So he's good."

"SEALs are always good."

"So you really think he is a SEAL?"

"I'd bet anything."

"Well... great. Just great." Her eyes were still closed as she let out a loose, shaking breath.

The blackness felt oppressive, closing in around them. Brenner had stood to his feet now and was pacing, holding his phone up above his head. He moved a few more paces down the tunnel then cursed.

"What?" she called out, though her voice felt faint in her own ears.

"Blocked," he said.

"The phone?"

"The passage. He knocked down another section."

"So..." she hesitated. "We're trapped down here?"

"No... No. *Yes!*" Brenner pumped his fist, still keeping his phone up with his other hand.

"Reception?"

"Yeah. It's weak. But I've got it. Calling now. They'll have us out in no time!"

Ella just nodded, still feeling light-headed and tired. She leaned back, resting against the stone, listening to the rushing water of the stream.

Brenner's voice joined the sounds a second later, as he excitedly exclaimed, "Yes. Yes, we're both fine. At least... I think." He shot an anxious glance towards her. "Hurry. Wait—how long? Hours? Why the hell hours? Get a back-hoe up here or something. Really? Shit... Okay. Well hurry!"

Ella didn't hear the rest of the brief, urgent exchange. Her mind was too caught up in her own thoughts.

Now that she was being put on time-out, against her will, her mind ventured forth, wandering.

The Collective.

She frowned, still leaning back. But her mind moved to a conversation with her sister in a hospital room.

To a conversation with a killer out at sea.

The Collective.

Some strange, sordid group... Somehow her father was connected to them. In his little book of blackmail she'd discovered, hints and clues had abounded.

She needed to know more about this secret society of killers. Who were they, exactly?

How long had they been operating?

She shivered.

How many people had died because of them?

It hurt her to think it, but she realized, with a slow, rising dread, if anyone could tell her about this secret organization...

It was Mortimer Graves.

The Graveyard Killer.

Another prickle exploded down her spine, bringing a sense of anxiety with it.

Her eyes fluttered, half closed, half open as she watched Brenner moving towards her, his form outlined in the dark.

He was still holding his phone up as he drew near.

She swallowed, hesitant.

Her mind raced. Her anticipation rose.

But it wasn't like she was *meeting* up with the serial killer again. A man who she'd allowed to escape custody. The reason, in fact, she'd been banished to Nome in the first place.

She'd sworn off ever interacting with him again... but would a small phone call really hurt anything?

She knew she was under some sort of investigation, or at least detailed oversight. But she'd labeled Mortimer Graves as a CI the last time they'd interacted.

It wasn't suspicious to call a CI.

Besides, she didn't even know if he'd pick up the phone.

She gave a stiff nod, reaching a decision.

She half extended a bruised hand, and in a hoarse voice, she said, "Can I borrow the phone?"

Brenner glanced down at her, still holding his device. He paused only briefly, but then, without question, he handed the phone to her.

The cold, metal casing and the smooth glass touched against her fingers as she lifted the device. No reception. She groaned, standing slowly.

Brenner shot a hand out, helping her up.

Now, standing, she spotted a single, faint bar of reception.

She swallowed, staring at the device. Then, from memory, she began dialing the number of Mortimer Graves.

"Who are you calling?" Brenner said.

"No one," she replied.

"Who's no one?"

"Just... just let me talk to him, okay? It's my CI."

"What CI? Graves? That weirdo?"

She shushed him, turning away to look the other direction. Partly so he wouldn't distract her, but also so he wouldn't see the guilt across her features.

Brenner didn't know who Graves really was. Ella had been lying to him, and now, she felt like something of a hypocrite, given their earlier conversation.

Still, the phone rang.

No one answered. She tapped her foot nervously, glancing down at the glowing screen to make sure she'd entered the correct number.

Finally, after what felt like an eternity, a strained voice answered on the other end in a clipped, polite, British voice. "I'm afraid I don't recognize this number. Who is this?"

Ella's heart raced as she listened.

It was the same voice she remembered. A smooth, confident voice. The voice of a man used to being in control.

A man, she knew, with dead eyes.

For a moment, she stood there, without responding. It wasn't too late to back off. Wasn't too late to shut it down... She didn't have to speak.

She didn't have to go through with it.

But the collective was out there. A mystery that she *needed* to solve.

So she cleared her throat, dabbing at her lips, which felt dry all of a sudden. Then she spoke. "Mortimer... it's me, Ella."

Silence followed her words, a thick and heavy weight that stifled her breathing.

"Eleanor," he said at last, his voice low and inscrutable. "To what do I owe this pleasure?"

She hesitated, unsure of how to continue. She had so many questions, so many things she wanted to ask. But there was also a part of her that wanted to keep her distance, to stay safe and out of harm's way.

"I need to talk to you," she said, finally finding her voice. "About the Collective."

She could feel Brenner watching her, his gaze burning a hole into her spine. But she didn't look back at him.

Couldn't bring herself to meet his curious gaze.

There was another long pause on the other end of the line, and Ella wondered if he had hung up. But then she heard his voice again, rough and gravelly. "I don't know what you're talking about."

"Don't play games," she said, her voice shaking with excitement. "Tell me the truth. Please," she added, true to form. She wasn't Priscilla. She didn't operate by entering every unknown situation guns blazing.

Ella held her breath, waiting for his response. Finally, he spoke. "You're playing with fire, Eleanor. You don't know what you're getting into."

"I don't care," she said, her voice rising in desperation. "I need to know."

A long pause. Then a curt reply. "Don't call this number again."

And he hung up.

Ella stared at the device, she tried calling again, but instantly received the dial tone.

"Shit!" she said.

"What?" Brenner asked. "Was that Graves? What's the Collective?"

"Nothing..." she said distractedly, trying to place the call again. But once more, all she was met with was a whining ring on the other end.

Then, as she tried again, a message said, *I'm afraid the number you are dialing has been disconnected.*

She blinked.

"Huh," Brenner said. "Guess he has some hard feelings after last time." The ex-SEAL chuckled, shaking his head, limping a few steps, then sliding down the stone wall to sit at her feet.

She huffed, glared at the phone, then handed it back to Brenner, sliding down as well until the two of them were sitting side by side, alone in the dark.

"Ass," she muttered under her breath.

"Who, me?"

"No, him. I mean... you too, sometimes," she added with a sniff.

He grinned, his white teeth flashing in the dark, his grayish eyes flickering from the glowing phone. "You don't mean that," he said.

"I do," she replied, still cross.

He was watching her closely now, and she could feel his gaze on her.

Suddenly, the silence seemed to surround them. The faint rush of the water was almost like a lulling noise.

Brenner paused, scratched at his chin, and he looked troubled now. He glanced off, and she glimpsed the usual expression of sadness she'd grown accustomed to seeing in his gaze.

Her heart panged in her chest. For a moment, it was as if her attention focused, and everything zeroed in. Briefly, she thought of it as tunnel vision and then winced at her subconscious' corny brand of humor.

"What?" Brenner said, noticing her expression.

"Nothing."

"Not nothing. You're lying again." But he said it in a teasing way.

She rolled her eyes at him, the glow from his dim screen providing the only illumination they had.

"Is it really going to take them hours to get us out of here?"

"Yeah. Whole tunnel collapsed."

"Great."

Brenner chuckled. "I mean..." he picked at the back of his hand. "I can think of worse things than being trapped down here with a pretty lady."

Ella felt her cheeks warm at this comment. But she was still watching him. The humor in his tone was evident, but the sadness in his gaze was also still apparent.

"How did she die?" Ella said, blurting the words out.

Brenner stiffened.

"Sorry," Ella said just as quickly. "I... not *how*. But... but... Are you okay?"

She winced.

Brenner wasn't looking at her anymore. Again, his eyes held that far-off quality. "I wasn't able to protect her," he said softly. "Five years ago. I was still on tour. She got in an accident."

Ella stared. "And... Priscilla?"

"Didn't think she could handle it." Brenner spoke stiffly, anger in his voice. "I mean... even before the accident, before she died... Priscilla wanted out. I could tell. She even mentioned putting her up for adoption."

"Oh... I see."

"Yeah, well..." Brenner was shaking his head.

"Is that why you started to drink again?"

Brenner shot her a sidelong look. He quirked an eyebrow. "What's gotten you so inquisitive all of a sudden?"

"Umm... Facing my own mortality in a cave-in?"

He snorted. "Fair enough. Yeh. But I haven't touched anything since... Well..."

"Since what?" she asked.

He closed his eyes and went quiet for a moment. She listened to the steady sound of his breathing. She reached tentatively out with one hand, her fingers touching his.

The moment she made contact, his eyes opened. He looked directly at her, and he asked, "What's the Collective?"

Chapter 17

Ella froze, caught off guard by the question. She stammered, shook her head, and then, in some relief, found she was able to answer honestly. "I don't actually know."

"Huh. Well... sounded serious on that phone call of yours. Who was that? Really?"

"My CI."

"I know when you're lying Ella."

She looked him dead in the eyes. "It was Mortimer Graves. I give you my word."

He held her gaze for a moment then nodded, looking away sheepishly. "Okay. And he's..." A swallow. "He's not... something else, is he?"

Ella froze, her heart pounding. Did Brenner know? She couldn't let him know. If he found out, everything was ruined. But she didn't like lying to him either.

She hesitated and then gave a non-answer.

"He's just a contact, Brenner. Nothing more."

Brenner gave her a skeptical look but didn't push the issue. "Alright, alright. I believe you."

Ella let out a sigh of relief, but the tension between them didn't dissipate. They sat in silence for a few more moments, the only sound being the trickle of water.

"Good," Brenner said at last. He seemed to relax. He shrugged and flashed a quick, nervous smile. "I was worried maybe he was something more."

Ella blinked. And then the inference struck her like a punch. "Mortimer? Something... NO! Hell no. We're not. He's not. Yuck!"

Brenner chuckled now at her reaction. If anything, he seemed more at ease now. "Damn. I touched a nerve."

She was shaking her head furiously, wincing as she did at the mere thought. "He's... it's not like that. At all. At *all.*" She cringed inwardly at the notion.

But Brenner seemed pacified. He was smiling contentedly, leaning back as he did, staring at the ceiling.

"Think we should give them another call?" Ella asked.

Brenner shook his head. "Gonna take them an hour to borrow a back-hoe and move it up the mountain pass."

"An hour just to get started?"

"Yeah."

"Great."

He looked at her. "You sure you're okay?"

"Positive. Stop asking. Please," she added sweetly. She reached out and flicked his ear.

But he caught her hand in his calloused, shooter's grip. He held her palm gently, his rough knuckles brushing her soft fingers.

They stared at each other for a moment.

"I mean..." Brenner trailed off. "I can think of a couple ways we might pass the time."

There was mischief in his eyes but also something else.

Ella realized now just how close they were sitting. How dark it was. How *alone* they were.

The smooth stone around them was padded with moss, and there was something almost idyllic about the meandering water through the granite.

"Really?" she said, returning his smirk. "At a time like this? You really do have a one-track mind."

"No," he said with a sniff. "I'm just... what was it? Contemplating my own mortality."

Ella snickered, shaking her head. Her hand was still held in his, and she didn't withdraw. He was leaning in now.

Such an odd thing, she realized.

The two of them were so often caught up in life-or-death circumstances, that it took a cave-in and a near-death experience just to give them some alone time.

He was leaning close, but waiting, as if hoping for her permission. She could feel his warm breath against her cheek. She smiled faintly.

He really was quite handsome.

Plus... plus, even if he hadn't been.

He was Brenner.

Brenner Gunn. It felt right, somehow, to be here with him. To be so close. She thought of all the pain he'd been through. Thought of the trouble he'd seen.

Her heart panged in her chest. She tried not to think too much of what Priscilla might think if she saw them.

It all seemed to fade in her mind. She leaned against Brenner, resting her head on his chest.

He kissed her softly, his lips grazing her forehead. She let out a long, contented sigh.

For a moment, it was as if they were the only two people in the world. The cave, the mission, everything else faded away. They were just two people in love, seeking comfort in each other's embrace.

Brenner's hand traveled up her arm, tracing circles on the soft skin of her shoulder. Ella shivered at the touch, her body responding to his gentle caress.

They stayed like that for a while, lost in each other.

But then Brenner's hand slipped lower, his fingers trailing down her spine. Ella gasped as pleasure shot through her body.

He leaned in to kiss her again, more urgently this time. His tongue brushed against her lips.

They broke apart, gasping for breath. Brenner's eyes were dark with desire, and Ella knew that hers were the same.

"Are you sure?" he whispered, his voice rough with emotion.

She nodded, unable to speak. Brenner pushed her gently onto her back, his eyes locked on hers.

For a moment they just looked at each other, taking in the sight of their beloved. And then he kissed her again, harder this time, his body pressed against hers. They forgot about the danger outside, the rest of the world, everything but each other.

Forgot about Priscilla. About Ella's family. The Collective. The Graveyard Killer.

There was so much to forget.

But as Brenner leaned in closer, Ella stopped him, her hand touching against his. They were both still clothed. She hesitated briefly then whispered, "Not yet. Not here."

She frowned to herself, wondering what she was doing. In a way, it took more from her to stop than it did to chase killers.

"Shit. Sorry," Brenner said quickly, sounding embarrassed.

But she shook her head quickly, still panting. "No... don't... don't stop everything. I mean. Just *that*. Not *that* yet. I don't have protection. Do you?"

Brenner blinked then blushed. He hesitated and shook his head.

Ella smiled at him, trying not to let him see where her thoughts had gone to. A child with Priscilla. A death. Brenner's broken heart.

She leaned in, this time taking her turn to push him back. Her body ached from the bruises, but she didn't stop.

"We can still have fun," she whispered in his ear.

And again, the two of them forgot the world as their lips pressed together once again.

Chapter 18

It had taken five hours for them to be dug out and another hour to return to the motel where they'd been booked.

And now, Ella's head rested against the motel room's pillow, exhaustion taking her completely.

She wanted to sleep. The red digital clock by the bed informed her that midnight had already passed.

It was as she was drifting off, though, that an urgent knock came at the door.

"Ella," Brenner's voice whispered.

She hesitated, blinking. Did he want to finish what they'd started back in that cave?

"Ella!" he said, louder.

She paused, then pushed from the bed slowly, approaching the door.

"The soil samples came in!" Brenner was whispering, hurriedly.

Ella's eyes widened, and she bolted forward now, pulling the door open quickly.

Brenner was standing there wearing a t-shirt and ripped jeans. His hair was tussled, and his eyes were wide with excitement.

His laptop was balanced against one arm, and he made a sweeping motion with it, as he hurried past her into the room.

Ella allowed him to pass before shutting the door behind him with a *click.*

As she did, Brenner was nodding quickly. "I think we might have something. I keep... keep thinking about that cop he took hostage."

"They didn't find any body," Ella pointed out.

"Yeah. I know. Which means he's probably taken the guy somewhere. A lair. Somewhere he's hiding out."

"And the soil samples?" Ella asked, trying to keep the yawn from her voice.

But Brenner was already nodding in excitement, his head bobbing up and down as he turned the laptop to face her. "We found high concentrations of magnesium and iron in these soil samples," Brenner said, his eyes gleaming with excitement. "These minerals are only found in certain areas, and I ran a quick search. It matches the profile of an abandoned mine located about fifty miles from here."

159

Ella's eyes widened as she grasped the implications of the discovery. "So, you think he's taken the cop into an abandoned mine?"

"If the sample is right... Like I'd mentioned, we had to rush it to get it back in time."

"Yeah... well, it's the only lead we have."

Brenner nodded, his face solemn. "We need to move fast."

Ella quickly got dressed, adrenaline pumping through her veins. She couldn't believe she was about to go on a rescue mission to an abandoned mine at the crack of dawn. But the thought of that helpless cop being at the mercy of a crazed criminal was enough to spur her into action.

As they made their way to their Jeep, Brenner explained their plan. "We'll take the fastest route to the mine and try to sneak in quietly. We don't want to alert him to our presence until we have to."

"I'll call backup."

"Sure. They can meet us there. Let's hurry."

Chapter 19

As they drove through the dark and winding roads, the mountains obscuring the rising sun, Ella couldn't help but feel a sense of dread wash over her. What if they were too late? What if the cop was already dead?

But she pushed those thoughts aside as she spotted the mine entrance ahead.

A sign out front warned trespassers to stay back, reading, "Danger: Abandoned Mine. Keep Out."

Ella and Brenner exchanged a quick glance before parking their vehicle a safe distance away.

"Sure we can't get closer?" Ella whispered as Brenner flung open his door and placed a boot out on the gravel road.

He shook his head, glancing off towards the base of the Alaskan mountains. "He's ex-Navy. Probably has the place rigged."

Ella shivered at these words and stepped from the vehicle as well. The shadows from the mountains, blocking out the sun, seemed to swallow them, surrounding them.

They quietly made their way towards the mine, their flashlights illuminating the dark path ahead. They could hear the sounds of water dripping from along rocky crevices, as hidden mountain springs wept; the echoes of their footsteps bounced off the walls.

As they approached the entrance to a boarded-up tunnel, they heard a faint sound.

Ella and Brenner both went still, staring in the dark.

The sound repeated itself, coming from just within the mineshaft entrance.

Ella glanced back. She could spot, far below, a small trail of emergency vehicles coming towards them, sirens off.

The wind was picking up, causing her golden hair to lash across her face.

She frowned, staring at the distant vehicles. It would take them another ten minutes, at least, to reach the pass.

Ten minutes that the hostage might not have.

She made up her mind, reaching the wooden boards, her fingers trailing along splinters and old nails. She pointed to a jutting piece of metal.

"Fresh nail," she whispered.

Brenner nodded but pointed up.

She glanced at where his finger was indicating. Then he pointed down. "Camera triggered by a tripwire," he whispered.

Ella stared. She hadn't even *seen* the gossamer strand across the base of the wooden boards crisscrossing the tunnel.

Brenner peered through the gaps of wood, moving his face towards the sound.

Ella's heart raced as they trained their flashlights ahead.

Suddenly, there was an eruption of movement. Scurrying steps. A small, bristling creature emerged under the floorboards, scampering between them.

A porcupine, with jutting quills.

Ella held back a yelp, and Brenner just stared. He shook his head in frustration, whispering, "Almost triggered the wire."

Then he reached out, cautiously, prying at the wooden boards.

With a quiet creak, the board came loose in Brenner's hand. He handed it to Ella and reached for another, his movements measured and careful. They worked in silence, slowly removing each board until they could see into the dark tunnel beyond.

Ella's pulse quickened as they peered in. It was pitch-black beyond the tunnel, but she could just make out a faint light in the distance. Brenner squeezed her hand, his own flashlight trained on the light.

"We need to move," he whispered. They avoided the wire stretched across the entrance, both of them ducking under a wooden board higher up.

Ella nodded at Brenner's comment, her heart in her throat as they stepped into the tunnel. The air was thick and musty, and the walls were slick with moisture. They moved slowly, their flashlights illuminating the way ahead. Another tripwire was just a few feet in, and they skirted it carefully, their eyes trained on the light in the distance.

As they moved closer, the light grew brighter.

"What do you think it is?" she whispered.

Brenner shook his head. "No clue."

"Does he know we're coming?"

Another shake. "No clue."

The two of them pushed forward, moving towards the glowing light until it cast their shadows as long streaks of ink behind them.

Finally, they reached the end of the tunnel, where the light was coming from. It was a small room, with a single bulb hanging from the ceiling. In the center of the room was a figure, tied to a chair.

Ella gasped as she recognized the cop they had been searching for. He was bruised and beaten but still alive.

Brenner started forward, but Ella held him back. "Wait," she whispered. "Something's not right."

The cop wasn't moving, his head hanging to the side. The man had red streaking down the side of his face, his eyes fluttering under the bright bulb above him as if he were still only half conscious.

He was trying to say something, his lips murmuring, but no sound was coming forth.

Brenner and Ella were tense in the doorway, then Ella spotted it first.

"His hand," she whispered. "See it?"

The cop's hand was trembling horribly. Shaking as if he were in an earthquake. His knuckles were white from where they wrapped around the ridged grenade he was holding, the pulled pin glistening on the ground under his chair.

"If he lets go of the grenade, we all blow up," Brenner whispered.

Ella looked further into the room but spotted no movement. Only bare walls and empty space.

The killer was nowhere to be seen.

But that didn't mean he wasn't here somewhere, watching them.

Ella felt her heart pounding hard in her chest as she considered their options. They couldn't just rush in and disarm the cop without knowing where the killer was hiding.

"Stay here," she whispered to Brenner. "I'm going to try and draw him out."

Before Brenner could protest, she slipped into the room, her flashlight trained on the trembling cop. She kept her movements slow and deliberate, her eyes scanning the room for any sign of the killer.

"Hey," she called softly to the cop. "We're here to help you. Can you hear me?"

The cop stirred slightly, his head lifting a fraction. His eyes met hers, and Ella saw the fear and pain in them.

"Just hold on," she said soothingly. "We're going to get you out of here."

She took a step closer, her eyes still searching for the killer. Suddenly, she heard a sound behind her. A soft footstep, barely audible over the sound of dripping water.

She spun around, her flashlight casting wild shadows on the walls. But she saw nothing.

"Ella?" Brenner's voice came from behind her, and she turned to see him entering the room cautiously. "You okay?"

She nodded, her eyes still scanning the room. "I heard something," she whispered.

Brenner frowned, his own flashlight trained on the cop. "We need to get him out of here before that grenade detonates."

Ella nodded, but she couldn't shake the feeling that they were being watched. She kept her senses alert as they moved closer to the cop.

His eyes were widening as she drew nearer. He kept shaking his head, desperately.

She paused.

He tried to speak, his voice creaking.

She heard another sound. A whimper.

"I'm sorry," the cop whispered. "He said..." a swallow. "He said he'd kill my family."

And then he reached out.

His hand wasn't tied to the chair. It had only looked like it.

He snatched at her sleeve, dragged her forward, and released the grenade as she tumbled into him.

Ella shouted in surprise as she fell, but even then, her instincts kicked in. As she toppled, she lashed out with the palm of her hand, sending the grenade skittering across the ground.

Brenner was already moving.

He was like a blur of color in the corner of her eye.

One moment, he'd been standing quietly in the entryway, the next he lunged forward, snatched the grenade off the ground, and flung it into the tunnel he'd just abandoned.

Brenner hit the ground next to Ella, covering her with his own arm.

They lay there, by the toppled chair with the weeping cop...

But there was no explosion.

No sounds at all anymore.

Ella breathed slowly, exhaling. Brenner looked up after a few seconds.

They remained motionless, quiet, staring towards the entrance to the room, neither of them moving.

Finally, Ella pushed herself up onto her elbows, her eyes scanning the room for any sign of danger. Brenner followed suit, keeping his arm protectively around her.

"What the hell just happened?" Ella breathed.

Brenner shook his head, his eyes trained on the entrance. "I don't know. But I can check."

He suddenly shot an angry glance back at the weeping cop. Brenner slapped the man across the face. "Cut it out. You were trying to kill us, asshole. Shut up!"

The cop was shaking his head, blood streaking his features. He kept whispering, "He knew their names. He said he'd kill them. He took my driver's license. He knew where I lived. I'm so sorry."

Ella felt a pang of sympathy in her chest, but Brenner wasn't as forgiving.

He slapped the man again as if trying to jar him to his senses and then hurried out into the hall. He returned with the grenade he'd retrieved.

As he drew closer, he muttered, "A dud. Too light."

Ella stared.

Brenner shrugged once then popped the top off the grenade. He shook it once, twice, and then a piece of parchment suddenly fluttered from inside the grenade, tumbling in a twirling motion to the ground.

Ella snatched the piece of paper, her breath coming quick, and she read a simple, handwritten note. *Stop coming after me. Or next time, it's real.*

She stared, feeling a cold tremble up her spine.

The cop was still crying, shaking his head.

Brenner gave the man another little shake. "When did he leave? Hey—hey, tell me when he left? What did he look like."

"I-I don't know!"

"How don't you know!"

"I didn't see him. I just saw his arm. He said if I looked at his face, he'd shoot me."

Brenner was scowling now. "Alright, so how long ago did he leave? Come on—spit it out!"

"I... Umm... About fifty minutes... Maybe?"

The man was wiping at his eyes, and glancing at the watch on Brenner's wrist, trying to read it upside down.

Brenner paused. "Fifty minutes? That's a pretty precise estimate, isn't it?"

The man shook his head adamantly. "Not an estimate!" he insisted.

Ella was still staring at the handwritten note. So casual, so cavalier... but why? Why go to such an effort? The grenade was... she glanced at it, her nose wrinkling, her mind spinning.

It was a prop. The note was a piece of artistic drama. It didn't make sense.

"What doesn't?" she whispered to herself.

Brenner glanced over at her as if to see if she'd been speaking to him, but then he returned his glare to the blubbering hostage.

But Ella wasn't paying attention to this. The posed victims, the bodies... the *vainglory*... It was all too much. And now this.

A step too far.

Mud on the boots that just so happened to lead to this cave? And what about the investigator coming in by plane? Someone had tipped off the killer...

Or...

Or someone on the *inside* had already heard the itinerary.

She glanced over towards the two men once more. She frowned as she overheard the next part of their conversation.

"I saw his watch. It was 1:00pm. Exactly."

"It said 1:00?" Brenner asked suddenly.

"Yeah. Yeah, it did."

"You're sure? It didn't say 13:00?"

"What?"

"Thirteen hundred hours," Brenner said now, and there was a note of something in his voice that sent chills along Ella's back.

"No... No, it said 1:00. I saw it!"

Brenner turned to Ella now, his eyes narrowed. He shook his head slowly.

"What's wrong?" she said.

"We've been wrong about this guy. We've been wrong the entire time."

Chapter 20

Deep within the heart of a dense forest, a winding path emerged, concealed by the thick foliage that surrounded it. The path, overgrown with twisted roots and scattered leaves, led to a secluded house—a dwelling veiled in mystery and seclusion. It was a place where the whispers of secrets mingled with the rustling of leaves, and the air clung with a sense of foreboding.

On this particular evening, as the sun above cast long shadows across the forest floor, a man emerged from the depths of the woods. His figure, clad in a tattered coat and worn boots, moved stealthily up the path, his presence as enigmatic as the night itself. A faint smile played upon his lips, concealed beneath a scruffy face that matched his unkempt appearance.

No-Name was smiling as he moved away from where he'd parked his truck. He whistled to himself, tossing a small, metal nail up and down in his hand. Up, down. He caught the nail, swallowed vaguely, and tossed it again.

He enjoyed lurking in the shadows like a phantom, his actions guided by a chilling purpose that was known only to him. His intentions, though concealed, were far from benign. Sometimes he was a mild-mannered shadow in the background.

Other times...

He was a Navy SEAL...

Though, not always. And not really.

He frowned, thinking about this. Thinking about the many names and identities he wore. He smiled again.

No-Name approached his hidden abode, a dilapidated house that seemed to blend seamlessly with the surrounding forest. Its windows were cracked, its roof sagging under the weight of time as if mirroring the dark secrets that resided within. The front door creaked open, revealing a dimly lit interior that hinted at a forgotten past.

Inside, the main room was sparsely furnished, illuminated only by the flickering light of a solitary lamp. A maze of dusty bookshelves lined the walls, their contents a testament to a twisted intellect. Trinkets and curiosities, some seemingly out of place, adorned every surface, casting eerie silhouettes upon the room.

Hidden away within the confines of this ominous dwelling, No-Name possessed a secret. A small screen, hidden in the wall. The screen displayed the images cast by a small camera, concealed in an inconspicuous corner nearly twenty miles away; it allowed him to peer into the activities back at the mineshaft. It was through this device that he watched, with an unsettling satisfaction, the actions of two federal agents, lost in the labyrinthine depths of his old haunt.

He'd led them there on purpose. He'd left them a message.

The pretty one with the blonde hair was reading and re-reading the message, shaking her head as she did.

The agents, their brows furrowed with concern, cast wary glances into the dark recesses of the shaft. Flashlights danced across the walls, their beams illuminating nothing but an endless expanse of gloom. They conversed in hushed tones, their voices carrying a tinge of anxiety that fueled No-Name's delight.

They were stumped. Just as they'd been before.

And as they'd always be.

They couldn't catch him.

They didn't even know him.

Within the house, a muffled sob reached No-Name's ears. His grin wavered, transforming into a grimace of annoyance. He strode toward the source of the sound—a small window, covered in grime, peering into the depths of the basement. There, huddled in the corner, a young woman trembled, her tear-streaked face pale and haunted.

"Quiet!" No-Name's voice pierced the air, sharp and authoritative. "Stop talking!"

The woman's cries subsided into choked sobs, her body quivering with fear. Her eyes, wide with terror, pleaded for mercy, but No-Name was deaf to her silent pleas. He paced back and forth, muttering to himself, the erratic movements of his shadow dancing upon the walls.

The woman was shaking her head, shifting. Her gown slipped, revealing the top of her chest, revealing the curve of her smooth skin.

He found himself staring.

And then he cursed, banging his fist into his own leg. Again, and again.

He waited until the pain lanced through him.

"Lust," he whispered to himself. "What would Mother say? Hmm... What would she say?" He was snarling to himself now.

And he tore his gaze away from the pathetic creature in the basement. As he did, his hand flashed across his vision. He spotted, on his back knuckles, the old wounds that his mother had once been forced to give him.

She hadn't wanted to.

She'd done it because she'd loved him.

Hurt him to train him. To discipline him.

He smiled in fond memory, one finger tracing the scars on his knuckles. His hand was clenched, the palm still aching from the pain of a shattered glass when he'd punished himself earlier.

"I've been trying to keep you alive," he said softly, glancing back at the woman. "Really... really trying. Mother would've wanted that. But you?" He shook his head, glaring at his sister. "You have no use. You do nothing. You're *slothful*."

She looked up at him, eyes wide where she was leaning back in the basement.

"I thought punishing you would be enough," he said, his voice stern.

She didn't look away, nervously swallowing. She tried to shift but stopped. Her leg was twisted under her, her ankle at an odd angle.

She'd injured herself a while ago and had stopped helping out around the house. She hadn't left the house in nearly a decade.

Their mother hadn't wanted her to.

The woman opened her mouth as if to say something but never managed to speak.

"Enough!" No-Name's voice grew shrill, a volatile crescendo of anger. "You've been at it for too long. Maybe it's your turn..."

His words hung heavy in the stale air as he descended the wooden stairs, each step creaking beneath his weight. A rusted doorknob greeted him at the bottom, its cold touch sending shivers down his spine. He grasped the handle, a gnarled hand enveloping it with a sinister grip, and swung open the door.

Within the bowels of the basement, a chilling silence waited. The only sound was No-Name's labored breathing, the anticipation of what lay beyond the threshold overwhelming his senses. As he stepped forward, a twisted smile contorted his face, an embodiment of the malevolence that consumed him.

His injured hand slipped into his belt, pulling out a thick knife.

Chapter 21

Ella kept glancing at the Marshal, and Brenner's left hand traced the scar along his chin. His other hand gripped the steering wheel as he drove rapidly through the dark.

"Explain to me again," Ella said softly, glancing over her shoulder from where she sat in the passenger seat to watch the cavalcade of police vehicles circling the entrance to the mineshaft. She glanced back towards where two officers were speaking with the captured cop.

She frowned and looked away again.

"I can't believe he didn't see the killer's face," she murmured.

"He was scared," Brenner said matter-of-factly.

Ella considered this, nodding once.

But then Brenner said, "I'm right about the watch."

"Explain it to me again. Because he used a digital watch?"

"No. Because he wasn't using military time. If he was a SEAL, he wouldn't function with 1:00pm. He'd function at thirteen hundred hours. It's like asking someone from the UK to explain inches and feet instead of the metric system. It wouldn't ever make sense."

"So what are you saying?"

"I... I don't know..."

Brenner's hands gripped the steering wheel tighter, his handsome features also rigid. He was staring through the windshield as they moved through a low bank of fog rolling through the mountains.

Ella's mind was still moving. She said, "Mud on the boots. But they were convenient to find... Would he really have been so careless?"

Now it was Brenner's turn to look at her, inching up an eyebrow.

Ella leaned back, brushing her golden bangs from her tired face. She caught Brenner staring a bit too long, and then he swerved, cursing, avoiding a branch in the road.

Ella's heart jolted, but she didn't comment on the distraction. Instead, she pointed at the road. "Exactly!" she said.

"Exactly what?"

"The ambush back at the airfield. Someone knew we were coming. Someone knew to ambush us a second time because they were listening. What if..." she paused.

"What?"

"What if the killer planted that emblem. The one from the SEAL team. What if he made it *look* like that to an outsider."

"But why?" Brenner said. "Why go to that trouble?"

"Because what if he knew *you* were going to be there."

The words hung heavy in the confines of the car. A faint whistling sound came from Brenner's window which was slightly cracked, allowing a breeze to gust through.

"How would he know anything about me?"

"Because," Ella said, biting her lip. She grimaced, not wanting to complete the thought but not certain how to do anything else. If she said it out loud, the whole investigation would change. If she voiced her doubts, it could be devastating.

But her instincts were telling her she was onto something. So she took in a deep exhalation and said, "I think the killer is a cop."

The two of them both went silent. It was as if an echo had filled the space. Brenner actually turned, still gripping the wheel, but his body angled now, his eyes fixated on her.

"What?" he said simply.

She winced but nodded. "Yeah... Yeah, I know. It sounds crazy. But... But I think I'm right."

"What do you mean, a cop?"

"Think about it!" she insisted. "And watch out—damn it. Watch the road, Brenner."

"I saw that cat."

"It was a deer."

"Whatever."

Ella frowned at him but then concealed the expression just as quickly.

He shook his head. "Don't do that."

She didn't have to ask *what*. He called it *lying* with her expression when she hid her emotions from him. She hadn't used to. Not when they'd been together all those years ago.

She sighed, frowned again, and then said, "The mud on the boots was processed in the same lab we sent out the APB from."

"And?"

"What if someone messed with the results? What if they wanted us to come here?"

"I don't get it."

"There were cameras. It was a setup. He's playing a game. All of this, think about it. There's a production to it. The whole thing is one big game." Now, as she spoke, Ella was picking up speed, her voice sounding thin and frail to her own ears, as if she couldn't contain her own excitement.

"Someone knew about our itinerary. And someone knew you were a Navy SEAL and that you'd be investigating with us."

"Hang on... What if they really are just a SEAL? Good at their job. Wiretaps, the lot."

"It doesn't make sense," she said simply, with a shrug. "You said it yourself. The watch. It's not the right time."

"Well... there could be other explanations. Maybe our friendly neighborhood hostage just misremembered."

"Maybe... But someone's been watching our every move. Someone's been killing indiscriminately. And what if the fact that those earlier cases *weren't* connected wasn't because of negligence..."

"But because someone intentionally tried to keep them hidden."

"Exactly."

"So you think it's a cop?"

"Yeah. And not just any cop. I think it's someone working in the precinct where we entered the evidence room."

"It... it's a theory..." Brenner said trailing off.

"You don't think I'm right?"

"I just... why would he pretend to be a SEAL? I don't get it."

"To mess with us? To act out some fantasy? Maybe... maybe he's never given that sort of respect in real life. Maybe that's why he kills."

"Maybe..." Brenner was biting on his lip, still frowning.

They picked up the pace, moving through the mist, racing back in the direction of the precinct.

As they sped forward, Ella realized what her accusations would mean.

They would have to solve this case on their own now. No help. No backup.

They didn't know who they could trust.

Chapter 22

Ella entered the precinct, moving quickly, her shoes squeaking against the floor in a sound that caused her to wince. But she didn't slow, moving with Brenner towards the desk sergeant.

"Excuse me," she said, leaning forward. "We need to speak with the officer who processed the mud samples from the high pass crime scene."

The sergeant gave her a wary look. "And who are you exactly?"

"I'm with the FBI," she said smoothly, flashing her badge. "It's urgent."

The sergeant hesitated for a moment before picking up the phone and making a call. She spoke in quiet, muted tones, glancing suspiciously at the two of them.

Then she shrugged, and glanced back at her computer, allowing the two of them to wait awkwardly. A few seconds later, a man came striding towards them, his eyes flickering between their badges and their faces. The man had a thick beard, and even thicker arms that strained under his suit sleeves. His eyes were ringed in red as if he hadn't slept in a couple days, but he stood tall and proud, tattoos just barely visible past the edge of his shirt.

"What's going on?" the large, tatted, and muscled man asked, his tone defensive.

"Are you the forensic officer who ran the mud from the high pass crime scene?" she asked.

"The one near the icefields?"

She nodded.

"Yeah. So what?"

"We need to talk to you in private," Ella said, glancing back at the sergeant.

The man frowned but gestured for them to follow him to a nearby interrogation room. As soon as they were inside, Brenner shut the door and turned to face him.

"Officer, we're investigating a murder that we believe you may have information about," he said.

The man's eyes narrowed. "That lady in the icefields? Or ladies, right... I haven't had a chance to check the second unit."

"Ladies," Brenner said, his eyes hooded, his face a mask.

Ella cut in. "We have reason to believe that the killer may have planted evidence." She didn't go so far as to accuse anyone at the precinct. At this point, it would only make enemies. And for all she knew, *he* was the one who'd done it.

She watched his reaction to her words, keeping a close eye on his expression.

But he didn't look nervous or scared.

Instead, the forensic tech let out a scoffing laugh. "You're kidding me, right?"

"We're dead serious," Brenner said, his voice low and dangerous. "And we're going to need you to tell us everything that went into analyzing that sample."

The man hesitated, his gaze flickering between them. Ella could see the sweat starting to bead on his forehead.

"I don't know what you're talking about..." he paused, wrinkling his nose. "I... I did what I always do. I ran the..."

He began to speak but then trailed off, frowning slightly.

Ella noticed this small aberration and instantly jumped on it. "What is it?" she said firmly. "Did you leave the evidence unattended?"

He paused, shrugging sheepishly. "I mean... I'm good at my job."

"We know," Ella said. "We already looked into your work schedule. You were working two of the nights victims were found. It's not you. We know that. But we need to know if someone bribed you. If you left evidence unsupervised."

"I mean... we're in a damn police station!" he said defensively.

"So you did?"

"Did what?" he asked.

"You're stalling," Brenner growled.

The techie threw up his hands. "Shit, I mean... Does a guy get to take a leak sometimes? I may have left the door propped open to the lab. No AC, man. The place gets sweltering."

Ella felt her heart sink. "So did you see anyone?"

"Nothing," he retorted. "At all!" he added. "And no, I'm not accepting no damn bribe. Do you know how much schooling it takes to get this job?" He was crossing his arms now, his tattoos more visible as his sleeves slipped back on his massive forearms.

Ella kept her expression neutral. Brenner might not like it when she didn't properly display her emotions. But this man wasn't Brenner.

"Okay," she said slowly. "But we still need you to tell us everything. Every detail, no matter how small it may seem."

"I already did," he said, his voice sharp. "I analyzed the mud samples from the crime scene and didn't find anything out of the ordinary."

"But you did remember something," Ella pressed. "You left the sample unattended. For how long?"

The man looked away, his face contorting with discomfort. "It's nothing," he mumbled.

Ella stepped closer to him, her eyes boring into his. "Tell us."

The man let out a long sigh, before finally giving in.

"Fine," he said, his voice low. "I left the sample unattended for a few minutes. When I came back, there was a note on my desk. It said 'Be careful what you find.'"

Ella's heart raced at his words. This was it. This was the break they needed. "A note?" she said, imagining the note back in the grenade. More melodrama. It was all a play. All make-believe.

"Did you touch anything after that?" Brenner asked, his voice tense.

The man shook his head. "No. I just finished up the analysis and put everything away. I thought maybe someone was playing a prank."

"Do you still have that note?"

"I mean... probably in the trash can. It was nothing. Just a note."

"Handwritten?" Ella asked, eager.

"No. Typed."

She felt her heart fall.

Ella couldn't help but feel a sense of disappointment. A typed note didn't give them much to go on. But it was something.

"Thank you," she said, her voice sincere. "We'll be in touch if we need any more information."

The man nodded, his shoulders slumping slightly with relief. As they left the room, Ella felt a sense of unease settle over her.

Brenner murmured at her side. "Dumpster diving?"

"Yeah," she whispered. "I want to see that note."

Chapter 23

Ella couldn't shake the feeling of unease as she and Brenner headed towards the precinct's trash area. They walked in silence, her mind racing with questions. Who had left the note for the forensic tech? And why would they warn him to be careful? If they wanted to avoid getting caught, wouldn't they want the mud sample to be contaminated?

As they approached the dumpster, Ella wrinkled her nose at the pungent scent of garbage. She watched as Brenner dug through the trash, his gloved hands sifting through discarded coffee cups and food wrappers.

After a few tense moments, he pulled out a crumpled piece of paper.

"Got it," he said, holding it up for her to see.

Ella's heart skipped a beat as she reached for the note. It was typed, as the forensic tech had said, but she could still make out the phrase "Be careful what you find" in bold letters.

"This doesn't make any sense," she muttered, studying the note, and wrinkling her nose as she held the fragment from the least soggy portion. "If someone didn't want the mud sample to be analyzed, why would they leave a warning? It's like they wanted us to find out."

Brenner nodded, his expression unreadable. "Maybe it's a diversion," he said. "They want us to focus on the note, so we don't notice something else."

Ella considered this for a moment, her mind racing with possibilities. "You're right," she said finally. "And it goes back to the more obvious question..."

Brenner stared at her, and the two of them remained quiet. Then Brenner said, "Do you really think a cop is behind all of this?"

Ella turned slowly, glancing at the precinct, her eyes fixated on the building. "Someone in there. Someone who had access. Yes. I really do."

Brenner looked at her, his pensive gaze intense. "Well..." Here he scratched at his chin. "Something keeps coming to mind.

"Oh?"

"Yeah. Officer Haver... he seemed pretty willing to go along with the whole grenade ploy. He looked scared."

Ella frowned. "What are you saying."

Brenner just shrugged, rubbing at his knuckles. "I mean... we're saying this guy is melodramatic. A killer who's worked for the precinct for a while, has access to evidence, and knew about the schedule of our flight coming in." Brenner looked at her now. "Officer Haver fits the entire bill."

Ella stared, picturing the man they'd "rescued" from the mineshaft. The same man who'd pulled the pin on a dud grenade. What if he'd *known* it was a dud. What if it was all one great act.

She said quietly, "We need to see if Officer Haver had any connection to the victims." Then, she added, "And we need to do it discreetly."

Brenner was nodding along at this.

They both knew that if Haver was truly the killer, they needed to approach this situation delicately. They couldn't risk tipping him off. The cops were still driving him back from the mineshaft, which meant for the moment, his desk would be unoccupied. Ella thought for a moment before coming up with a plan.

She turned to Brenner on the steps outside the precinct.

"Let's split up," she said, her eyes fixed on Brenner. "You go talk to the victims' families and see if they remember seeing Haver around. I'll stay here and see if I can find any evidence linking him to the murders."

Brenner nodded in agreement but then hesitated. "You sure? I can stick around."

"I'm fine. Just be back by the time he returns."

Brenner scratched at his chin but then gave a sigh, shrugged, and turned. "Sounds like a good plan," he said over his shoulder, heading towards the parking lot. Ella watched him go before turning to head back into the precinct.

She knew she had to be careful. If Haver was truly the killer, then he would do everything in his power to cover his tracks. Ella made her way through the hall, nodding politely at the desk sergeant. She needed to find Haver's desk, though she wasn't familiar with the precinct.

She couldn't ask either, not without tipping off his colleagues.

Her gaze moved along the various doorways, searching for the placards on the wood.

She paused after a few steps, peering down a short hall that dispensed into an office area. A conference room was unoccupied at one end of the room, and a small smattering of cubicles littered the gray carpeted floors.

Cops were sitting in desk chairs. Others were moving towards a printer, while still another was on his phone, gesticulating agitatedly as he spoke into the receiver.

Ella nodded politely as a detective hurried past her. The man didn't even glance in her direction, so she strode forward, casting her gaze about, searching for any evidence of Officer Haver's desk.

"Come on," she murmured to herself. "Which one's yours...?"

Her gaze slid over a framed photo in a cubicle to her right. But the figures in the image were unrecognizable.

She shook her head, and moved faster, her gaze sweeping back and forth in rising desperation.

Then she saw it. A small plaque with Haver's name on it mounted on a desk at the end of the room. She moved forward, gliding past the other detectives unnoticed, and approached the desk.

She hesitated only briefly, her hand grazing the thin, upholstered divider separating the cubicles. She glanced surreptitiously back, making sure she was unnoticed, and then she slipped into the cubicle, moving quickly.

Chapter 24

The cubicle in question had an impressive view of the Alaskan wilderness through the window. Verdant spruce and fir trees stretched for miles, creating a bewitching canopy that seemed to extend endlessly. Beneath the boughs, along the distant mountain slopes, Ella could just make out the azure tread of winding creeks with bubbling brooks meandering through them. The sun set on this sublime landscape, painting the sky in hues of pastel pinks and purples.

She turned away from the window, her attention diverted to the desk.

The desk wasn't nearly as eye-catching.

It was cluttered with paperwork, a computer, and a coffee mug that had gone cold. Ella glanced around the room to see if anyone was watching her, and then began sifting through the papers on Haver's desk.

She felt her heart pounding in her chest, the thrill of the hunt coursing through her veins. She found nothing at first, just paperwork related to previous cases and phone messages from colleagues. She was just about to give up when she saw something that made her heart skip a beat.

A small bracelet.

She stared at the band of beads and metal.

Her eyes moved to the photographs under the computer screen. The bracelet was a woman's size. There were no women in Haver's family photo.

She returned her attention to the bracelet, lifting it, and staring at the item. Her memory was often one of her greatest tools.

Growing up, she'd spent time memorizing flags, license plates, and phone numbers. She could still recite Pi to twenty digits.

But another memory was tugging at her. Did she recognize that bracelet?

She frowned.

Bit her lip, then pulled her phone out, scrolling to the first victim's social media profile. She clicked on the first profile picture, her frown deepening as she glanced at the bracelet once more.

The beads on the bracelet were identical to the ones in the profile picture. She zoomed in closer and could just barely make out the faint initials etched into one of them. "M.T."

Her heart was racing now, the pieces falling into place. This was it. She had found the evidence she was looking for.

But she couldn't get caught. Not yet. She stood up, slipping the bracelet into her pocket, and quickly made her way back towards the main hall.

She needed to confront Haver, but not here. She needed to lure him out, where she could interrogate him without tipping off his colleagues. She sent a quick text.

Forget the follow-up. Meet me in the parking lot.

She hesitated briefly, staring at her phone, willing that Brenner hadn't left yet.

Then... a speech bubble.

You sure?

Yes, she texted back.

And then she moved slowly back down the hall, her heart pounding. What if the bracelet was just a mistake? Maybe there were many bracelets like it... but what were the odds of that?

The corpse of the victim *hadn't* had the bracelet. So why did Haver have it on his personal desk, under some papers?

A memento?

She shivered.

As she stepped out of the precinct, she saw Brenner emerging once more from his vehicle. He stepped back, watching her and leaning against his car, his arms crossed. He looked up as she approached.

"What did you find?" he asked, his eyes hardening as he took in the expression on her face.

"We need to go," Ella said, not bothering to answer his question. She was already pulling open the passenger side door, her eyes scanning the precinct for any sign of Haver in the parking lot.

But the officer hadn't yet returned from the mineshaft entrance. Perhaps they'd even taken him to the hospital.

Brenner hesitated for just a second before getting in the car.

"What's going on?" he asked again.

Ella stared straight ahead, her grip tight on the steering wheel as she pulled out of the parking lot. "Haver had a bracelet on his desk that matched the bracelet of our first victim," she said finally, her voice barely above a whisper.

"Well... what if he was just analyzing it as part of the investigation."

But Ella shook her head. "No... Not possible. The bracelet wasn't found with the body."

Brenner leaned back now, watching her. "So... how do you know it belonged to our victim?"

"Because," she countered. "I remembered it from her social media posts. She was wearing it. But not when we found her."

Brenner's eyes widened. Then, just as quickly, his expression hardened. "What's the plan?"

"We can't speak to him here. He has too many allies. We need to catch him en-route. Speak to him on the side of the road if we have to."

"Cops will be with him," Brenner said.

"We can handle a couple. We just don't want to be surrounded by a hostile precinct."

Brenner nodded, turning the key in the ignition. "I have the GPS of the incoming squad cars here," he said, nodding towards where his phone rested on the dash, displaying three flashing red lights.

Ella nodded in approval. "Good. Very good. Let's go. We can't let them get by us, Brenner. We need to make sure they stop."

"You're sure it's him?"

"I'm not sure of anything. But I'm sure we need to speak to Haver again. This time not as a victim, but as our prime suspect."

Brenner was shaking his head, his expression dark.

Ella felt the same emotions.

The two of them both knew the ramifications of kicking over this hornet's nest.

A cop was the killer?

Even the whiff of an accusation could tarnish his reputation. Could also lead to reprisal... retribution.

Hell... Ella had once seen her own sister use a shotgun in the middle of a precinct.

She winced, trying not to get ahead of herself.

They needed to intercept Haver's car. They'd then speak to him... more directly than the last time they'd spoken.

If he was the killer...

She frowned.

She was confident she could see through a ruse this time.

Chapter 25

The trees whipped by around them in a blur of green and brown.

And with each passing second, Ella felt her heart hammer.

She peered through the windshield, scanning the mist-veiled roads ahead.

A fog bank had rolled in from the icefields, obscuring the road as much as twenty feet ahead.

"How far?" she asked.

"He's a minute out," Brenner said, his voice tense.

Ella nodded, her eyes glued to the road. They had to do this right. They had to catch Haver off guard, before he could call for backup. Before his escort could stop them.

As they rounded a bend, Ella spotted the familiar flashing red lights in the distance. "That's him," she said, her voice barely above a whisper.

Brenner's knuckles whitened as he clenched the steering wheel, his foot pushing down on the gas with an intensity that shook the car. Inching closer to Haver's car, Ella rolled down the window with a trembling hand, her gaze fixed on the driver. The air around them felt thick with the rolling fog.

Ella rolled down the window the full way, then shouted, "Pull over!" Her voice rang out through the quiet mountain pass. "Pull over! We need to talk!"

A police officer in the front seat looked over at them in confusion. Ella could feel her heart pounding in her chest as he slowly shook his head, pointed at his watch, and then tried to veer around them.

But Brenner moved, keeping pace with them, trying to edge them slowly off the road.

The cop car began leaning on its horn. The sound buzzing in the still air.

"Pull over!" Brenner's voice boomed through his open window as wind whipped through.

But the driver kept leaning on its horn, trying to veer around them again. The man driving was gesticulating at them angrily. Clearly impatient.

Or was something else going on?

She couldn't see into the backseat. Was Haver there? Did he have a weapon?

Her mind darted back to his own hostage situation.

The car ahead of them was speeding up now, refusing to slow.

They had to do something.

Ella knew they had to act fast. She reached behind her seat, her hand closing around her pistol. Brenner noticed the movement and nodded, reaching for his own weapon. The car was now dangerously close to the side of the road, the dirt and rocks threatening to send them tumbling down the mountainside. Ella raised her pistol, aiming for the car's tires, trying to disable it.

The shot rang out loud and clear, the sound echoing through the mountains. The car swerved, spinning out of control, and then screeching to a halt on the side of the road.

Ella and Brenner slammed on the brakes, skidding to a stop beside the overturned car. They quickly got out, weapons at the ready, and approached the stalled vehicle.

"Hands up! Come out with your hands up!" Brenner was shouting.

At first, there was no response.

Then, a figure emerged, scowling, flinging open the front door.

"What the hell?" the figure demanded.

It was the escort. No sign of Haver just yet.

But he didn't look like someone taken hostage. Instead, he was standing with his hand on his holster, glaring at the two of them, his eyes blazing.

"You trying to get us killed?"

"Is Haver in there?" Ella demanded.

The cop hesitated, staring at her, frowning, then glancing briefly back into the car. He wrinkled his nose and looked at her again. "You're the fed."

"Yes! Now move your hand from your weapon, sir. We need to speak with Officer Haver, please."

The cop's expression soured. "What the hell do you want with Haver?"

Ella tightened her grip on her pistol. "We need to question him about the murders."

The cop's eyes widened in shock. "What? That's absurd! Haver would never do something like that!"

Brenner stepped forward, his own weapon held steady. "We'll be the judge of that. Now where is he?"

The cop hesitated for a moment, then gestured towards the back seat of the car. "He's back there."

Ella and Brenner exchanged a look, then made their way towards the back of the car. As they reached the rear door, they could hear Haver's muffled curses and grunts coming from inside.

Ella grabbed the door handle and pulled it open, revealing the cop sitting with his hands tangled in a seatbelt, trying to pull it free. His face was red, his eyes darting back and forth between Ella and Brenner.

"What the hell is going on here?" he spat.

Ella didn't respond. Instead, she leaned in close to him and said, "Officer Haver, we have reason to believe that you weren't honest with us back there."

Haver's eyes widened in shock, then narrowed in anger. "That's bullshit! You've got no proof!"

"Proof of what?" she said. "I just told you I thought you were dishonest. Proof implies... guilt of some sort, doesn't it?"

She spoke calmly, coldly.

But now, he was blinking, staring at her, his mouth agape. "I... I..." He trailed off, his nostrils flaring.

He looked scared. Trapped.

And then he flung himself forward.

Brenner shouted.

Ella lurched back.

Haver hit the parking brake and flung his body against the seat ahead of him, causing the car to rock, to tilt, then begin to slip forward, down the incline on the side of the road.

Ella managed to lunge back, avoiding the swerving bumper of the runaway car as it sped down the hill towards the row of trees at the base of the steep incline.

A second... two...

Then *crash!* The vehicle slammed into a tree at the base of the hill, sending glass erupting in a small geyser.

Chapter 26

"Ella, careful!" Brenner shouted.

But she was already moving. Sometimes, she didn't just *throw* caution to the wind but launched it into a typhoon.

And now, adrenaline coursed through her thin, petite frame as she hopped the barrier on the side of the road and broke into a dead sprint down the steep incline.

Ahead, in a blur of motion, she watched where Haver was scrambling out of the vehicle.

He was gasping, blood streaming down his forehead.

But he glanced back, through the swirling fog, his eyes widened, displaying the whites like China dishes, and then he turned, sprinting off into the woods.

Ella nearly stumbled from just how acute the angle of the incline was.

The lower she went, her feet thumping against the knobby grass, the thicker the fog became until she could barely see ten feet ahead of her.

"Officer, stop!" she shouted.

But it was to no avail. She could hear him ahead of her, amidst the trees at the base of the snow-laden mountain. Could hear his heavy breathing, his stumbling footsteps, his gasps.

But she couldn't see him now. The twenty feet of visibility from the road had turned to more like ten in the thick forest.

She had to slow, moving more cautiously now as the ground angled out. She circled around the side of the smashed vehicle.

The bumper was indented, and glass littered the front seat.

She didn't call out now.

She noticed that there was an empty holster laying in the passenger seat.

No gun there. A spare holster? Or had Haver taken the weapon?

Now a slow prickle of fear moved down her spine.

But Ella wasn't one accustomed to giving in to fear. She frowned, moving slowly in the swirling fog, and she moved forward, darting ahead once more through the dark, breathing heavily.

She could hear the cracking of twigs and the rustling of leaves ahead. Haver was close. And it sounded like he was moving fast. She was close behind him, but her feet were struggling to keep up with the slippery slopes. Ella stumbled and nearly fell face-first onto the rocky terrain, but she managed to regain her balance by grabbing onto a low-hanging tree branch. She looked up and saw a flash of movement ahead of her.

She pushed forward, her heart thudding in her chest as she closed the distance between herself and the fleeing officer. Her mind raced with questions. Was this as good as admitting his guilt?

He'd run.

Why run?

Why hadn't the car stopped?

She broke through the thick foliage and into a small clearing.

And then she saw him. Haver. His back was turned to her as he fumbled with something in his coat pocket.

"Freeze, Haver!" Ella shouted.

But he didn't listen. Instead, he pulled out a revolver from his pocket, spinning around to face her.

Ella drew her own weapon, feeling the weight of it in her hand. She had trained for this. She could handle it.

But the sight of Haver's finger on the trigger of his gun sent a shiver down her spine. She didn't want to kill a man.

"This is your last warning," she said, her voice steady. Inwardly, she was a tangle of nerves and fear. Ella's poker-face might have irritated Brenner, but it was useful in moments like these.

She displayed no emotion, just cold, calm certainty. Her gun held in steady hands.

"If you point that thing at me... this is over," she said softly.

His revolver was still aiming off to the ground. He was looking at her, exhaling deeply.

A low whimper crawled from his throat and burst into the clearing. The fog swirled around him.

"I know..." he whispered quietly. "I know what you're going to do."

"And what's that?" she pressed.

He watched her, his eyes wide, his gaze flicking past her, up the slopes. "I know what you are," he whispered even more fiercely.

She frowned now, staring at Haver. "What are you talking about?"

He didn't reply.

"What I am?"

"I know what *you* are!" he snapped.

She said nothing. Just stood there, his eyes locked onto hers. He was still gripping his revolver, pointing it at the ground.

She could tell by the look on his face that he wasn't going to back down.

Seconds ticked by like hours. The two of them just stared at each other, weapons drawn.

And then, without warning, Haver lunged forward, his gun aimed at Ella's chest. He'd hoped by darting *in,* he might distract her.

But she had already seen him tense. Had read his intention.

The moment he lunged forward, so did she. But to the side, angling away from him. His gun had to sweep in a wide arc, but before it could, she covered the final few steps between them in those ten feet of visibility.

The fog danced and snapped and twirled around them like a whirlpool as she sidestepped his attack and, using her training, took him down with a swift kick to the chest.

He groaned, stumbling back. But he held his gun. He tried to raise it again.

She'd decided not to shoot. She needed to know if any other victims were out there.

Needed to confirm what she'd suspected.

And so she moved in again, devoid of fear as if having drained it like pus from a wound.

She didn't allow the fear to enter. Didn't allow it to seep in.

She lashed out with the palm of her hand, bringing it into his wrist. The gun clattered to the ground. He lunged at it, pinecones crunching underfoot from his sudden movement.

She struck again.

Her foot slipped on the uneven ground, knee buckling as she struck him in the face.

He stumbled, his upper body lurching back, and he groaned. She regained her wobbly balance, darting forward again.

She couldn't let him gather his sense.

Ella reached for her handcuffs.

But as she did, he dropped suddenly.

His hand lashed out. She tried to strike, but he caught his gun, rolling in the detritus, covered in pine needles and bits of smashed pinecones.

He was gasping, his face streaked with sweat.

And then he reached his feet.

But instead of pointing the gun at her...

He was aiming it at his own head. Breathing in and out rapidly, his eyes wide, his nostrils flaring.

Behind her, Ella thought she heard Brenner's voice, calling for her in the misty forest.

But she didn't turn. Didn't speak. Instead, her entire focus was on Officer Haver.

"Sir," she said quietly, holding out a hand, "Let's talk about this. Lower the weapon, please. It doesn't have to end like this."

He stared at her, and then his lips twisted in a sneer. His face was gaunt, bloodied. His head wound was still oozing crimson.

"I know what you are," he said, in a breathy voice. He was staring at her as if he'd seen a ghost.

"Sir... I..." She frowned. Was he just trying to confuse her?

But the gun pressed against his own temple wasn't confusing at all. The safety was off. If he pulled that trigger, he would decorate the branches and boughs with brain matter.

She licked her lips nervously. One hand still clutching her own weapon, but her other reaching out as if trying to keep the man calm.

She spoke as soothingly as she could. "I found the bracelet on your desk."

He blinked. "What bracelet?" for a moment, he just looked confused.

This mirrored her own emotion. "The one you took when you killed your first victim of Vainglory. We know all about it. Are there others? People you're holding somewhere?"

He was gaping at her now as if she'd slapped him. He blinked as if uncertain whether he was awake or asleep.

Then, he let out a little snicker. "You're serious? That's your play? To gaslight me? I should've known... I knew you were involved. But it didn't click until you'd left!"

Ella hesitated. "Wait, what?"

He was still pressing his gun against his temple. None of this made sense. He thought *she* was involved?

"I'm not going to let you torture me!" he yelled, his voice wobbly. "I won't do it! I'm not scared of death!" he said, but the squeak in his voice and the hesitation of his index finger suggested otherwise.

Ella's mind was still racing to try and make sense of all of it.

But she had to keep him calm.

"We haven't done anything to hurt you," she said in a soft, gentle voice.

He barked out a laugh. "Oh, but you have. And you don't even know it. All those people, the ones you killed... the bracelet? There was no bracelet!" He was incoherent. Nothing he said was making any sense.

"No bracelet? Sir, I found it on your desk."

"You planted it there!"

"You're saying someone is trying to frame you?"

"No. I'm saying you are! I read up on you, Ella. I know all about it. Your father! I know about them. And... and I know about the Collective. I know your sick, twisted game."

213

His words caused her to go completely still, and she froze. Her mouth opened, then closed again, and her eyes narrowed.

"What do you know about the Collective?" she said, momentarily distracted.

"Nothing. What? I... Nothing. I'm sorry I said anything. I just... please don't hurt me! I'll shoot myself if you come close! I know what sort of things you do to your victims. I've seen it!" he said, his voice hoarse.

He choked on his words, his mouth clamping shut before he could continue speaking. His eyes shone with tears, which he hurriedly blinked away.

"Please," Ella said, her voice full of confusion, "Put the gun down. You don't have to do this. We can help you. We can..."

She trailed off as he shook his head, his gaze never leaving her face.

"No one can help me. I should've seen it before. You knew the itinerary of the plane. You knew the plan to lure the killer out. You knew about the evidence locker. It was you all along. And your Marshal boyfriend. You're the killers!" he yelled, his eyes flaring.

And now it suddenly made sense.

He wasn't bluffing. Wasn't gaslighting.

He was just wrong.

But he thought he was right. It was why the car hadn't slowed for them. He must've told his theory to the other officer, telling him not to stop or they'd be tortured.

He knew about Ella's father's connection to the Collective. She barely knew about it.

But this man... he thought she was here to torture him to death.

He suspected her as much as she suspected him.

But now... now a rising sense of doubt came over her.

If he really thought she was the killer... then how could *he* be? Unless it was all an act.

She was staring at him now, studying his every move. "I'm not the killer," she said quietly. "And I do know about the Collective, but barely."

"Liar!"

"I'm not lying," she said. "But I can't tell... if you are." Had the bracelet really been planted? Had someone else in the precinct tried to frame Haver?

He took a deep, shuddering breath, his eyes full of terror. He thought she was the killer. She had to convince him otherwise while also finding out if he had an alibi. Something to prove his own innocence.

It wasn't an ideal location for this conversation, trapped in a forest, with mist swirling around them.

But it was the only backdrop they had.

Beggars couldn't be choosers, especially with a man threatening to blow his own head off.

She spoke evenly, with calm words. "Please... I'll lower my gun if you lower yours. We can go back. Nothing happened to your partner. Brenner, the marshal, is with him right now. We can call the precinct. See? You can tell them your suspicions about me. Here, look, you dial."

She'd pulled her phone from her pocket, deciding that she had to solve the crisis one step at a time before unraveling the confusing twist.

She handed her phone towards him, extending it.

His one hand still gripped the gun against his head, but his other tentatively probed out to accept the device.

He stared at it then up at her as if confused.

"It has reception. Barely. Now call. Look, I'm not going to shoot you. Just call. Would someone involved in any of this allow you to do that? Go ahead. I won't stop you."

She waited patiently, watching.

His face was pale. And then, suddenly, his finger tightened on the trigger.

And a gunshot rang out.

Chapter 27

Haver fired into the air three times. The loud blasts echoing around them. He shouted out now, "Landon? Are you there!"

His voice shook as he called into the fog, his words probing the darkness. A pause, and then an answering voice. "Haver? Haver, where are you? Did she shoot you?" came the reply.

"N-no, I'm fine!" he called back. His voice shook with emotion.

Ella glanced back to see Brenner and Landon emerge from the mist, moving cautiously in the treacherous terrain.

"Hold on!" snapped Haver, his gun still gripped tightly, but aiming at the sky. His wide eyes kept glancing towards where Ella's own weapon remained pointed at the ground.

"I didn't have anything to do with this," Ella said slowly.

"And you think I did?" he retorted.

Now, Brenner and Landon had emerged. Landon was holding his hands out, trying to speak swiftly. "Haver, it's not them. Gunn here showed me his phone—they're looking into this. They really are."

"We found a bracelet belonging to one of the victims on your desk," Brenner cut in. "Care to explain it?"

"There was no bracelet," he retorted.

Haver was trembling, but again, Ella couldn't quite tell if it was all a mask.

Brenner clearly didn't believe the man. He was glaring at the gun still pointing at the sky. "You need to come with us," Brenner insisted, his voice something of a growl.

"No! No, you'll kill me. Are you Collective too?"

"Am I who?" Brenner said.

Ella grimaced. She quickly cut in, hoping to redirect the conversation. "Look," she said, "Do you have any proof it isn't you?"

"That's not how it usually works, is it?" Haver snapped. "Innocent until proven guilty, right?"

Ella sighed, shaking her head. "I know. I'm not trying to throw you in jail. I'm just trying to clear your name, if in fact, you are innocent."

"You think he's innocent?" Brenner said sharply, nudging her, his tone hesitant.

She just shrugged, giving a quick shake of her head.

Brenner was now frowning again. The tension only seemed to mount as everyone exchanged uncomfortable glances.

The cop, Landon, looked at Haver hesitantly, frowning. Brenner was clicking his fingers, taking a step forward, limping only slightly, and gesturing at Haver. "Put the gun down, then. Come on."

But the officer looked hesitant. He was shaking his head, nervous. Suddenly, his eyes widened, and he blurted out, "Do you really think I kidnapped myself?"

"We think maybe you set it up," Brenner replied. Then, glancing surreptitiously at Landon, he said, "And maybe you had some help."

Ella was still frowning. Was she being played? She tried to study Haver's expression, tried to read his panicked gaze, wondering if it was all a facade.

Landon seemed to have realized what Brenner was implying now. He turned sharply, causing the mist to swirl. The four of them were like hunched shadows in the woods. All of them standing resolute like sentry towers.

But now, Landon scowled at Brenner, the mist swirling about him under the dark, yawning canopy. "What the hell, man? You think I'm somehow in on this?"

"I didn't say that," Brenner shot back. "I'm just saying Haver probably had some help."

Ella was shaking her head now. "Unless it wasn't him."

Brenner looked sharply at her.

She winced and shrugged.

She looked back over her shoulder. Hesitant.

"You have an alibi?" Brenner demanded, turning his gaze back to Haver. "Hmm? Anything?"

The cop was still breathing heavily, still wearing his look of panic.

Ella's mind continued to race. She didn't think it was him... He seemed genuinely terrified. And while their killer had a penchant for melodrama... he wasn't a coward.

It was the Vainglory, the Lust, the other deadly sins that she couldn't allow herself to overlook.

The killer had a very strong moral code.

He was merciless, ruthless.

Not a coward...

No.

And Haver was either playing the part... or she was right. It wasn't him.

She looked back in his direction, frowning slightly, then she opened her mouth to say something.

But before she could, there was another gunshot.

This time, coming from behind them.

Brenner reacted first, flinging himself at Ella in a split-second, trained reaction, his instincts taking over as he brought the two of them crashing to the forest floor.

Haver wasn't nearly so lucky.

He lurched back, stumbling into a tree. He blinked a few times, mouth unhinged.

And then a red stain blossomed across his chest, spreading.

Landon yelled, lunging forward. "Shots fired! Shots fired! Officer down!" He was screaming into his radio receiver. But then, a second later, he cursed.

He was kneeling at Haver's side, glancing around in fear, panting heavily like a startled doe. He kept touching his fingers to his radio but then cursing. "No reception? How the hell is there... jamming... Someone's jamming us."

Ella was still trying to disentangle from under Brenner's muscled form. The two of them were still close to the ground as they listened to the wheezing, gurgling sounds coming from Haver.

There was another loud *crack,* and a tree branch above them shattered, sending leaves curling down towards them.

The echoing shot was like some death knell, and as Ella pushed hesitantly to her knees, crouching behind a thick trunk, breathing heavily, she felt a cold, dreadful certainty that whoever was shooting at them was aiming to kill.

Chapter 28

Ella shivered in the mist, watching furtively in the dark.

Brenner pushed himself up, his gun aimed in the direction of the gunshot. "We need to move," he said, his voice low and urgent.

Ella nodded, already in a crouch behind her tree cover. Landon was still trying to rouse Haver, his face twisted in fear and frustration. His fingers were stained red where he was pushing at his companion's arm.

But Haver wasn't moving.

Wasn't breathing.

His own gun lay off to the side, discarded.

Brenner took charge, grabbing Landon's arm and hissing fiercely, "Arterial bleeding. Straight shot through the chest wall, out the back. The heart is ruptured. He's gone. We aren't. We need to get out of here. Now."

As always, Brenner didn't speak in such a way to spare feelings. His voice was firm, determined.

And yet Landon seemed to react to it, nodding a couple of times, wiping his hand off on the grass, still low in the mist.

Crack!

Another rifle shot resonated through the woods. This time, Ella didn't see where the bullet impacted.

The one benefit of the mist, which obscured her vision, was that it also seemed to be hampering the shooter's aim.

"Come on!" Brenner whispered again, more fiercely, gesturing towards the officer.

Landon hesitated, seeming torn. But then, another gunshot rang out, and he surged to his feet, leaving Haver behind.

Brenner and Ella followed quickly, bolting. Brenner squeezed off a couple of shots for covering fire.

Temporarily, the rifle gunfire subsided.

The three of them sprinted through the forest, scrambling over fallen logs and ducking under low branches.

Ella could feel her heart pounding in her chest, her breath coming in gasps as she ran. She could hear the sound of her own footsteps, the pounding of Brenner's boots beside her.

But then, there was a sudden snap, and she went tumbling forwards. She cried out in surprise, the breath knocked out of her as she hit the ground hard.

Brenner spun around, his gun trained in the direction of the sound. But there was only the rustling of leaves and the distant sound of rushing water.

"Ella?" he said, sounding panicked.

She groaned, pushing herself up onto her elbows. Her knee was throbbing, and she could feel a trickle of blood running down her shin. "I'm okay," she muttered, shaking her head to clear it.

Brenner moved closer, wrapping his thick arms around her to help her stand. "We can't stay here," he said...

Landon was glancing at them wide-eyed, horrified.

Ella stared at the man. He had blood on his hands and kept glancing at it. They didn't know much about him.

He'd said the radio was jammed...

But could she verify that?

These troubling thoughts disappeared, however, as Ella stared at her feet.

There was another cracking sound but this time, not from gunfire.

In fact, for a moment, all thoughts of the gun were put on the back burner as Ella realized what she'd tripped on.

Ice.

A thick chunk of ice jutting from under a tree root.

And the ground ahead of them, a long, sharp glaze of cold ice. This portion of the forest looked as if it had been flooded by spring swell, the water trapped before the freeze eventually came.

The half-submerged, forested area gave way to a larger lake, also frozen.

It was directly ahead of them and also blocking off any further movement in that direction.

"We have to go back," Landon was saying, his voice shaking horribly.

But before Ella could reply, there was another gunshot.

The ice exploded at her feet, sending chips of cold up, spitting at her face.

"Come on!" Brenner commanded, not waiting for protests.

He pulled at her, tugging Ella onto the ice.

She followed—it wasn't like there was anywhere else they could run to.

The killer had a larger weapon. Could somehow track them in the mist. Had the element of surprise and the upper ground.

They needed to move, to find a more advantageous terrain to protect themselves.

But now, as they moved over the submerged, half-frozen forest, she began slipping.

She and Brenner moved slower now, their feet sliding on the slick ice.

Behind them, Ella thought she heard the crunch of footsteps echoing in the mist.

The cold, clinging air swirled around them, falling across the ice, even as she stumbled and slipped across the treacherous terrain.

As they stepped onto the frozen surface of the lake, a thin layer of ice cracked beneath their weight, sending an ominous shiver through Ella's body. The sound echoed across the stillness of the evening, a haunting reminder of the danger that lay ahead.

They moved cautiously, their steps measured and deliberate. The ice creaked and groaned beneath them as if whispering warnings of the treacherous path that lay ahead. Ella's heart pounded in her chest, her senses heightened to the eerie silence that surrounded them. She tried to keep low, to move swiftly but carefully, praying desperately that the mist would hide them from the rifleman.

Suddenly the silence was shattered by a sharp crack followed by the whizzing sound of a bullet slicing through the air. Panic gripped Ella and Brenner as they dove to the ground, instinctively seeking cover behind a small mound of snow. They were being hunted.

The mist enveloped the lake, obscuring their vision. They strained their ears, trying to pinpoint the source of the gunfire, but all they could hear was the sound of their own heartbeats thundering in their ears.

Brenner gave a low whistle, and Landon joined them in the snowy mound, panting.

Another shot ricocheted off the ice nearby, and Ella and the others froze, waiting for what seemed like an eternity for the sound of more gunfire. But eventually, the echoing cracks faded away.

"He's repositioning," Brenner whispered sharply. "I can see him. He's not a SEAL. He's giving up a better perch to get closer."

Brenner was frowning now. Ella couldn't see any of the things Brenner seemed to.

The mist was again still, the eerie silence returning to the lake.

"We need to go," Brenner said, his voice low but strong.

The three of them peered through the mist, trying to discern their route. Slowly, almost hesitantly, they began moving on the ice again, wary of another gunshot.

They moved low and swift with purpose, only the crunch of the ice beneath their feet indicating their presence.

"Wait, no!" Brenner said sharply. "Phones away. Phones away!"

But Landon had been pulling his device out, and the small screen illuminated their space.

Ella's eyes widened as Brenner tried to knock the phone free.

But then, there was another *crack*.

In the midst of her spiking fear, a cry of pain pierced the air.

Ella whirled around, eyes wide, staring.

Landon had been hit.

He struck the ground, bleeding.

Two more shots followed, but Ella and Brenner had ducked, hiding in the mist again.

Brenner didn't stop, didn't slow, but instead began inching back towards Landon.

She followed, wincing at the sound of his moans of pain. Ella and Brenner crawled toward him, their bodies low to the ground, desperate to reach their wounded companion. The cold bit at her fingertips and ate through her clothing with a frigid dampness.

The mist seemed to thicken, obscuring their view further. Ella's heart ached as she saw Landon clutching his bleeding side, his face contorted in agony. Brenner scanned the mist, his eyes darting in every direction, trying to locate the shooter. Ella glanced back too. And then she thought she spotted a faint glimmer of metal through the haze, a rifle barrel protruding from a hidden vantage point.

Brenner had seen it too. His own gun raised. He fired back.

And Ella heard a curse. The rifle vanished.

"Hurry!" Brenner whispered.

With trembling hands, Ella tore at the hem of her own sleeve. Their first-aid kit was back in the stalled vehicles. She pressed a makeshift bandage against Landon's wound, trying to stem the flow of blood. "Hold on," she whispered, her voice laced with urgency. "We're going to get you out of here."

Brenner, his face set with determination, was still whispering, his gun trained at the spot where she'd spotted the shooter. "We need to move now. Ella, you take Landon's other side. We'll drag him to the tree line."

As they began their desperate crawl through the mist, the unseen shooter continued to rain bullets down upon them. Each shot sent shockwaves through their already fragile resolve, but they pressed on, driven by the indomitable will to survive. Ice exploded around them.

And an entire chunk of the thick cold suddenly tipped, like an iceberg, tipping and revealing the churning water beneath.

Gasping, Ella lunged, avoiding this sudden crater beneath them.

Ella's muscles strained as she dragged Landon's limp body across the ice. The weight felt unbearable, and her fingers grew numb with the effort. She glanced at Brenner, his face etched with pain, yet fueled by determination.

The shore was only fifteen feet ahead.

Ten.

Another gunshot.

Something stung across her shoulders. But it had missed.

Five feet.

Landon was no longer moaning. No longer moving.

She felt a flash of guilt that she'd been suspicious of him.

And then, another gunshot, just as they were about to reach the shore...

And the ice beneath them cracked, sending Ella into the cold... under the surface of the frozen lake.

Chapter 29

Ella's heart pounded in her chest as she fought against the biting cold. She was trapped beneath the frozen ice, her body suspended in the frigid water. Her lungs screamed for air, and she knew she had to break the surface or drown. With every fiber of her being, she pushed forward, her body slicing through the water with desperate determination.

The anticipation built as Ella's muscles burned from the effort. The ice above her seemed impossibly thick, a cruel barrier between her and salvation. She kicked harder, her legs thrashing in the freezing water as her hands reached out, searching for any weakness in the icy prison that held her captive.

As seconds stretched, Ella's vision blurred with the cold. Her body shivered uncontrollably, threatening to drain her last reserves of strength. But she couldn't give up. She couldn't succumb to the suffocating darkness that threatened to engulf her.

Finally, after what felt like an eternity, Ella's fingertips brushed against a hairline fracture in the ice. Hope surged through her, fueling her determination. She clawed at the frozen surface, her nails digging into the brittle ice, as she fought to widen the crack. She could feel the water tugging at her, the current pulling her further and further away from where she'd first entered the river.

She managed to scrabble her fingers against the ice, and her mind flitted back to a memory of diving under water for gold in her first case back in Nome.

But this time, she wasn't wearing an oxygen mask.

The ice groaned and cracked under her relentless assault. Ella's heart soared with the knowledge that freedom was within her grasp. With one final burst of energy, she kicked upward, propelling herself towards the expanding gap in the ice. The cold water seemed to cling to her body, trying to drag her back down, but she fought against it, her mind laser-focused on the air waiting for her above.

As Ella's head broke through the surface, the rush of cold air filled her lungs, invigorating her weary body. She gasped for breath, her senses overwhelmed by the sweet taste of oxygen. But her victory was short-lived.

The sound of a gunshot shattered the air, and Ella's heart skipped a beat. Panic surged through her as she realized she was not alone.

In the brief instance she glimpsed the shoreline, she realized she was very much alone...

The current had taken her far from where Brenner was trying to save Landon. She couldn't even see them along the waterway. Now, she realized why the ice had managed to give. It was thinner here, with spiderweb cracks lancing through the ice, like pitchforks of lightning, giving a maze to traverse.

As another gunshot rang out, her heart thundered.

With a renewed sense of urgency, Ella forced herself to dive back into the icy depths, aiming for one of these spiderweb cracks in the ice, trying not to be jostled under the ice once more. The water enveloped her once again, its icy tendrils biting into her flesh. She kicked and swam, searching desperately for a place to hide away from the unseen shooter's line of sight.

Each stroke was a struggle, the numbing cold sapping her strength with every passing second. She fought against the urge to gasp for air, knowing that a single breath could betray her position. The pressure in her chest grew unbearable, her lungs screaming for relief.

Ella's heart hammered in her ears as she fought against the water's resistance. She couldn't see the shooter, couldn't anticipate their next move. All she could do was keep moving, keep swimming, and pray that luck would be on her side.

Bullets whizzed through the water, creating trails of bubbles as they pierced the surface. Ella's instincts took over, guiding her towards a jagged outcrop of ice. She pressed her body against the frigid surface, using it as a shield against the shooter's deadly aim.

Time seemed to slow as the shots continued to ring out. Ella clung to the ice, her fingers growing numb from the cold as she fought against the crushing weight of exhaustion. She couldn't afford to make a sound, couldn't afford to give away her position.

But she couldn't stay here.

Couldn't breathe. Her skin was going to get frostbite. Hypothermia was likely already setting in.

But these other thoughts suggested potential risks, whereas a bullet to the head was an immediate death sentence.

Survival depended on her ability to stay hidden, to stay alive.

Minutes stretched into an agonizing eternity as Ella waited for the gunfire to cease. Her body trembled with a mixture of fear and cold, threatening to betray her presence. But she remained still, her breathing shallow and controlled as she listened for any sign of the shooter's retreat.

Finally, the shots subsided, their echoes fading into the distance. Ella dared to hope that her tormentor had given up, that she could finally emerge from her icy refuge.

With trembling limbs, she pushed away from the jagged ice and swam towards the surface once more.

As Ella's head broke through the water, she sucked in a gasp of cold air, relief flooding her senses.

She gasped, her throat aching from the desperate pulls of air.

But the danger still lurked, the icy waters and the unseen shooter waiting to claim her life.

Her body ached, her limbs heavy with exhaustion, but Ella refused to give in. She had come too far to surrender now. With every ounce of strength she could muster, she propelled herself through the water, searching for safety, for warmth.

She reached the shore, rising slowly to her feet, trembling.

And then she heard a click.

She was alone.

No sign of Brenner.

No sign of Landon.

No sign of civilization at all.

Instead, she found herself staring up at a figure in a hood, wearing a very large, dark, wooly coat.

His face was hidden in shadows. But his gun pointed at her head. She noticed his knuckles were bruised and scraped.

"Don't look at me!" he screeched.

She looked down.

She dripped water onto the shore, trembling horribly. She needed to get warm. Needed new clothes. A fire.

But now...

None of that would happen.

The gun pressed against her head, and the man above her gave a nervous, little giggle.

"I got you," he whispered. "Oh yes, I got you."

Chapter 30

The icy wind whipped through the barren landscape, carrying flecks of snow that stung Ella's already chilled face. She was soaked to the bone, huddled against a jagged rock on the side of a frozen river. Her trembling fingers reached tentatively towards the handgun pressed to her temple, its metallic chill a stark reminder of her precarious situation.

The man loomed over her, his face obscured by a low hood and a collar pulled high. His large coat billowed in the biting gusts, lending an air of menace to his already formidable presence. He sneered, his voice dripping with sadistic glee.

"You thought you could best me, didn't you? You thought you had me. How vain can you be, hmm? Vanity is a sin. Didn't you know that? Didn't you!" His voice screeched, then returned to a low giggle. "Looks like your luck has run out. Any last words before I color the snow in pretty reds?" He paused, as if thinking, then murmured, "Have you ever noticed how the ice crystals dance in the wind? It's... it's beautiful."

"Beautiful, yes!" she said suddenly, swallowing. "And you're a purveyor of beauty, aren't you?"

She still wasn't looking up. She could feel the gun against her skin, the cold metal pressing tight. She was still trembling, freezing where she knelt.

Ella's heart pounded in her chest as she surreptitiously surveyed her surroundings, her mind racing for a way out. She had been caught off-guard, but she refused to succumb to fear. With a steady voice, she replied, stalling for precious seconds. "You don't have to do this. We can work something out, can't we? I'm not vain. I promise you."

"Not humble, either," he said. "And with that clothing clinging to your frame like that... You're trying to arouse lust, aren't you?" He chuckled, wagging a gloved finger in front of her. "But no... No, I won't be tempted."

"Who are you?" she whispered.

He snickered, his breath forming puffs of frost in the frigid air. "Oh, Ella, always the optimist. You think you can talk your way out of this, don't you?"

He knew her name. He knew a lot. He was a cop from the precinct, so how come she didn't recognize his voice?

She tried to glance up, to get a look at his face, but then thought better of it, and reverted her gaze to the ground.

He was still prattling, quite content to hear the sound of his own voice. "But you see, I've waited a long time for this moment. Revenge is a dish best served cold, they say. And what could be colder than this?"

Ella's eyes darted to the frozen river beside them. The ice shimmered in the pale light, its surface cracked and treacherous. She knew she had to buy herself some time, create a distraction. With calculated precision, she feigned hesitation, her gaze shifting to a point behind the man. She shivered a final time, waiting for him to draw breath to continue speaking.

And it was as he drew a breath that she moved.

There was no time to think. No time to wait.

She was sick of men like this.

Men like her father.

Those who thought the world bowed to their whims. That they were the arbiters of justice...

Most humans who thought of themselves as "good people" had to be careful not to become cruel or self-righteous.

But a man like this?

He'd become drunk on his own ego.

And now she was alone, facing another predator. She thought of the phone call Graves had dodged. Of these whispers now following her, concerning the Collective.

Brenner was nowhere to be found—this was all on her. It was all the opportunity Ella needed. She lashed out with her free hand, striking his wrist with a swift, unexpected motion. The gun slipped from his grasp, tumbling through the air before disappearing into the freezing depths of the river.

Without missing a beat, Ella sprang into action. She brought her knee up into the man's gut, doubling him over in pain. Her hands, trained to deliver lethal strikes, found their mark on his exposed jaw, cracking bone against bone. The resounding impact echoed through the desolate landscape.

But the man was a formidable adversary, despite his momentary vulnerability. He retaliated with a vicious swing of his massive arm, catching Ella across the face. Blood mingled with the rivulets of melting snow on her bruised cheek, fueling her determination. She ducked and weaved, evading No-Name's lumbering strikes with a dancer's grace.

He was taken aback by her sudden fury but now seemed to recover. He growled, lunging at her but missing. His eyes flashed under his hood.

She dodged his first strike. Her mind whirled with anticipation, each move a calculated response to his every action. She feinted, drawing him in, before sidestepping with a fluid agility that belied her petite frame. With a swift kick to the back of his knee, she sent him sprawling onto the frozen river's edge.

Desperation fueled their struggle as they grappled in the unforgiving cold. The man's size and brute strength posed a formidable challenge, but Ella's cunning and training held the key to her survival. She used every trick in her repertoire, exploiting his vulnerabilities with precision strikes to his joints and sensitive areas.

Their fight became a chaotic ballet, the sound of their exertions blending with the howling wind. Ella's fists became a blur of motion, delivering blows with unerring accuracy and causing the mist to twirl above them. The man, his face a mask of rage and frustration under his hood, veiled in shadow, countered with raw power, each of his strikes shaking the ground beneath them.

Finally, as the exhaustion threatened to consume her, Ella found an opening. She sidestepped a blow and brought her knee into his stomach, sending him stumbling back onto the ice.

He yelped as he slipped and tried to regain his feet.

She stood breathing heavily on the shore, glaring at him.

"Don't move!" she snapped.

But he didn't listen. Instead, with a faint whimper, he tugged at his hood, still hiding his face.

Then he turned on his heel and began to run, slipping and sliding across the ice.

She was breathing heavily, trying to gather her wits. And then she burst into action without hesitation. It was like standing on the edge of a cliff, a paraglider attached, waiting for the initial jump. Like peering over a steep bridge at dark waters below before diving.

Like the moment before confronting a serial killer in his lair.

She'd trained for such moments.

The thought of being alone. Isolated. Her weapon water-logged, her figure shivering and cold...

It didn't compute. None of it registered.

She didn't care about the fragile ice across the lake top. She didn't take the time *to* care. She just ran, fog streaming from her mouth with each panting breath.

Ella felt her heart race as she chased the man in the hood across the desolate, frozen lake. The biting wind whipped at her face, numbing her skin, as her boots slid precariously on the icy surface.

Evening had subsided, and night had replaced it. She hadn't even noticed this happen, but now, the pale illumination clued her in. The moon hung low in the sky, casting an eerie glow over the barren landscape. Ella's breath came out in short, white puffs as she fought to keep up with her elusive target. Her mind raced with questions: Who was this man? She hadn't recognized his voice.

Was she making another mistake? She shivered. She'd been so distracted.

As she neared the center of the lake, the man in the hood glanced back, his eyes hidden beneath the shadow of his hood. There was a glimmer of amusement in his gaze—a twisted game he was relishing.

With renewed determination, Ella pushed herself harder, her boots crunching against the ice. The lake stretched out before her, vast and unforgiving. The thought of falling through the frozen surface into the frigid depths below sent a shiver down her spine. Already, she was trembling violently. Already she couldn't feel her feet or fingers. Her clothing stuck to her, freezing her. She couldn't go much longer like this.

But as if reading her thoughts, the man increased his pace, his long strides covering the ice effortlessly. Ella's heart pounded in her chest, and she willed her legs to move faster. She couldn't let him escape; too much was at stake.

Suddenly, a crack echoed across the frozen expanse, and Ella's heart skipped a beat. Panic set in as the ice beneath her feet splintered, sending spiderweb fractures in every direction. She stumbled, her arms flailing for balance, but managed to stay on her feet. The near brush with danger only fueled her determination further.

In the distance, the man in the hood disappeared into a dense copse of trees. Ella sprinted towards him, praying that she wouldn't fall through the treacherous ice a second time.

But her legs were locking up.

She stumbled onto the shore, amidst the mist. Her hands were trembling. Her legs gave out, refusing to continue, her feet too numb. Would she lose toes?

She thought, briefly, of her younger cousin Maddie. They'd had a lunch date they'd been forced to postpone more than once. Maddie had lost a toe to frostbite.

Ella lay on the ground, gasping into the leaves, beneath the fog, on the shore. The freezing cold had caught up with her now.

She was alone, isolated in the wilderness.

The sound of fleeing footsteps had faded now.

No further sign of the fleeing man in the hood. No sign of anyone.

And it was in this moment that the adrenaline fled. Ella simply lay there, motionless, gasping, and desperate.

Ella's body trembled uncontrollably as she lay on the cold, icy riverbank outside Juneau, soaked to the bone. Her teeth chattered with each shallow breath, and her voice quivered as she called out desperately.

It was a difficult thing to do... to call for help.

She'd lived a life trusting her own instincts and her own skills.

There was nothing wrong with the confidence born of competence, but it became a vice when it turned to self-reliant pride.

Ella had always hated the pride of her family...

But it taxed her in ways that troubled her to raise her voice, desperate, calling like some mewling kitten in the mist. "Brenner!" she cried, her voice carried away by the harsh Arctic wind. "Please, Brenner, I need your help!"

Her clothes clung to her body, trapping the cold against her skin. Ella's heart thundered in her chest, her mind racing with thoughts of frostbite and hypothermia.

As she called out again, the tension in Ella's voice grew, her words laced with desperation. The stakes were high—time was slipping away, and the biting cold threatened to claim her.

And then, a faint voice reached her ears. "Ella? Ella, is that you?" Brenner's voice was filled with concern and relief as he drew closer to her. He was also breathing heavily, suggesting he hadn't stopped running for some time.

"Yes, Brenner! Over here!" Ella's voice cracked, hope surging through her despite the numbing cold. She strained her eyes, searching for any sign of her friend.

Moments later, Brenner emerged from the snowy landscape, his breath visible in the frosty air. Panic lined his face as he took in Ella's shivering figure.

"Are you okay? Are you shot?"

The only energy she could muster allowed her to give a brief shake of her head, her teeth still chattering. Without wasting a second, Brenner sprang into action, gathering firewood and clearing a small area on the ground.

Ella watched him, her heart swelling with gratitude and warmth despite the icy chill that gripped her. Brenner was always there for her. There was an unspoken connection between them that had survived the freeze of more than fourteen years.

As the flames licked at the tinder, Brenner turned his attention to Ella, realizing the urgency of the situation. Gently, he helped her undress from her cold, wet clothes, his touch sending tingles through her body. In that moment, their shared vulnerability took on a new dimension, a hint of something more.

Brenner swiftly removed his own coat and draped it over Ella's trembling shoulders, his body warmth seeping into her skin. The gesture was simple, yet it carried a profound weight. Ella remembered a similar moment they had shared before, when their connection had teetered on the edge of something more, but nothing had come of it.

"We need to stop meeting like this," she said, her voice shaking. She tried to brush it off, to make light with a laugh.

But Brenner was just frowning, his own muscled and scarred wrists visible without his coat which now draped over her.

As Brenner continued to tend to the fire, Ella mustered the courage to lean in closer to him, seeking solace and comfort. His presence was a lifeline in this frigid wilderness, thawing the ice that had settled around her.

With the fire crackling, Brenner knelt down beside Ella, his hands gently cradling her cold feet. His touch was tender, his fingers working to restore circulation and warmth. Ella closed her eyes, allowing the sensation to wash over her, grateful for his steady, unwavering presence.

"What happened to Landon?" she whispered.

Brenner looked up at her, frowned, then shook his head.

"He didn't make it?"

Another shake. "Lungs. Vitals. Bled out. I couldn't help him."

Ella briefly had a biting, terrifying thought.

Was it that Brenner *couldn't* have helped Landon, or was it that he'd chosen to come after her instead?

This thought tormented her for a few moments as she considered the implications.

But then she swallowed, shaking her head, still trembling, and leaning against Brenner's warm form once more.

His hands continued to rub at her feet, returning circulation.

Another dead cop.

Ella felt the bitter chill of this thought.

Haver. Dead.

Landon. Dead.

So who was the man who'd taken shots at them?

Who was the real killer?

But her mind refused to go this route.

She just sat there, trembling as Brenner tended to her feet. Then moved on to her hands. Still rubbing, still helping her warm.

She continued to tremble, but less violently this time.

In that moment, time seemed to stand still. The world around them faded into insignificance as the connection between Ella and Brenner deepened. The fire's warm glow danced in their eyes, mirroring the flickering flame of desire that had ignited between them.

As the fire blazed, it was not only the cold that was melting away. Ella realized that this time, she wouldn't let their shared vulnerability go unspoken.

And as the warmth returned to Ella's body, radiating from her feet to her core, she found she could breathe a bit easier.

She wore nothing under his coat. Her mind was foggy, she knew that.

But the killer was long gone.

They had no way of calling for backup until they returned to their car.

And in her current state, she wasn't sure she could take ten steps, no less make the trek back to the vehicles.

"Brenner?" she whispered, her breath soft against his ear.

He didn't turn. Didn't speak at first. He was busy tossing another branch onto the fire. Sparks swirled up, rising higher and higher.

"Brenner?" she whispered again.

"Hmm?"

"Are you okay?"

He looked at her, his blue-gray eyes studying her from his handsome face. He didn't look away, the fire illuminating the side of his familiar features.

Features that were as much a fixture of her history, her existence, as her imagination.

How often had his countenance existed in her thoughts?

Perhaps it was brain fog from the exhaustion, the cold. Or maybe it was the heightened emotions of the near brush with death, the escape.

But there, shivering on the shore, in the mist, with no one to watch them, Ella felt as if she had tunnel vision.

Her ears were perked. The killer was long gone. He'd fled. Likely back onto the road, perhaps even stealing one of their vehicles.

They were truly alone.

Strange things happened when two souls found themselves completely isolated from the world.

Strange thoughts occurred.

Though, perhaps, not so strange.

She leaned in, her lips brushing his cheek.

He didn't withdraw.

Her fingers moved up, caressing his hair, touching his cheek. Ella's heart was beating fast, the adrenaline from their near-death experience still coursing through her veins. She knew this wasn't the time. They needed to recover. Needed to escape.

"Ella, Ella wait," he whispered. "We need to get you warm."

She gave a soft chuckle, her eyes still half closed. "So let's get warm," she said. She was unable to resist the pull between them any longer.

Brenner paused at her words. Then he turned his face towards hers, his lips hovering just inches away from hers. She could feel the warmth of his breath on her skin, and anticipation and desire coursed through her like wildfire.

In one swift motion, Brenner pressed his lips to Ella's, and she gasped in surprise. His kiss was urgent and hungry, his hands pulling her closer to him. Ella responded eagerly, giving in to the heat that was simmering between them.

Their lips moved together in perfect harmony, their bodies pressed together, and the fire crackled behind them. It was like they were the only two people left in the world, and nothing else mattered but this moment.

Eventually, they pulled away from each other, both breathing heavily. Brenner looked into her eyes then leaned his forehead against hers. Ella could feel his breath hot against her skin, and she shivered with desire.

"I've missed you for so long," Brenner whispered, his voice rough with emotion. "I... thought... you might be taken from me permanently this time."

"Never," she said, her voice a whisper. She knew it was a promise she couldn't keep. But in a way, those sorts of promises took the most courage when done for love.

Ella smiled. Her teeth were no longer chattering. "Me too," she replied softly.

And then she leaned in again, this time pressing her body against his more insistently.

He yielded to the pressure, rolling back onto the detritus, leaves crinkling and rustling under him.

Ella straddled him, her fingers working at the buttons of his shirt, eager to feel his bare skin against hers. The fire was larger now. The cold was pushed back as if they had their own little oasis of warmth.

Their bodies moved together, the rhythm of their motions in sync. It was a dance between two people who knew each other's movements by heart.

Their faces were illuminated by the flickering fire, and she could see the look of adoration in Brenner's eyes. It was a feeling that was mirrored in hers, and it was one that she hoped they could hold onto, even when they had to return to reality.

Eventually, the intensity of their lovemaking subsided, and they lay there, spent and exhausted, tangled up in each other's arms.

The fire continued to rise... It was as if it were growing even brighter, rather than burning to embers, though, she tried not to read much into this. The blaze cast long shadows across the forest floor.

They lay under a blanket of jackets and clothing. Ella's skin pressed against Brenner's. Her soft chest against his muscled, scarred figure.

The crackle of the fire, the warmth of his company was almost enough to make her forget.

In the shelter of the mist, in the forest, it was like a small slice of fiction.

A momentary reprieve from the cold, harsh reality that lay on the other side of those trees...

But she couldn't forget the killer.

Couldn't forget the victims.

Couldn't forget one other thing, too.

He knew their faces.

They didn't know his.

This wasn't over.

Chapter 31

Ella didn't shiver so much now as she leaned back in the rescue helicopter's seat, staring out at the scenic Alaskan wilderness below.

Long stretches of green trees stretched out before her, interrupted only occasionally by clear, blue lakes and the occasional snow-capped peak. The helicopter's pilot was skilled, swooping through narrow channels and around looming cliffs with practiced ease.

But there was nothing at ease about Ella's mind. It had taken the rescue team five hours to find them. Another hour to extricate them.

Now, Brenner was sitting at her side, his hand touching hers. She didn't pull away, and the two search and rescue operatives didn't comment on the apparent bond.

Ella was just so tired of always considering what other people thought.

She'd often said to herself that one caught more flies with honey. But now she was just too tired.

She held Brenner's hand. A sweet, affectionate touch.

Just like things had once been.

And perhaps how they were once again.

Her head leaned against his shoulder now, and the whir of the helicopter blades above echoed in her ears.

Vaguely, she could just discern the shouted questions directed at them by the rescue team.

"How did you get out there?" one was barking. "What happened to Officer Landon? Haver?"

But Brenner was replying in short, curt sentences.

The pilot kept glancing into the mirror. Another police officer had come with the group, sitting next to the pilot.

The man up front had a scowl and a thick beard.

The bearded, scowling man was the one that tipped her off to something untoward.

His hand was on his gun.

He had two sets of handcuffs sitting on the floor at his feet. She'd caught a flash of metal, leaned in, pretending to yawn, and spotted them.

Two pairs of cuffs.

She frowned now, glancing back towards where Brenner was shaking his head, and saying, "What do you mean? You think we *wanted* that to happen to Haver? The idiot pulled a gun and pointed it at his head. Then was shot by the *real* killer."

"And who might that be?" came the loud response, competing with the helicopter blades.

Brenner just shook his head.

"Beats me if I know. Isn't that your job?"

Ella frowned now, feeling a rising sense of doubt. The next comment by the rescue operative sealed it.

"We received an SOS not long before the murders. Officer Haver accused *you* of being the killers."

Ella tensed.

Brenner had gone quiet. Now, he also seemed to notice the way their security guard up front was fingering the trigger on his Glock.

Brenner swallowed faintly, licking at his lips.

"He was wrong," Brenner said simply. "We were all wrong."

"You don't mind answering some questions, do you?"

"I already am, aren't I?"

"In a more formal setting," replied the bearded cop, leaning back, and glancing over his seat once more.

Now, Ella's stomach was a bundle of nerves.

Were they under arrest?

She knew it didn't look good. A man had accused them of murder then had ended up dead after they'd rammed his vehicle.

Another officer, the only other witness, had also been killed.

Their story of another shooter, who they hadn't identified, clearly wasn't swaying hearts and minds.

The helicopter began to dip, moving through the mountains. And now, below, Ella spotted Juneau. But her eyes weren't drawn to the sprawling coastal city or to the waters lapping against the shore.

Rather, her eyes were fixated on the ungodly amount of flashing lights and emergency vehicles waiting for them at the small airfield strip.

The landing pad of the helicopter was covered in a swarm of cops.

She shivered.

"Shit," she whispered.

Brenner shook his head, still glaring at the men questioning him.

Ella could feel the tension in her hands. Her fingers were still numb, and it would take some time for full feeling to return.

But if they were arrested... If they were forced to sit through interrogations, it meant no one was out there... finding who'd really done this.

And who was likely going to do it again. Maybe even sooner now, knowing that he'd just escaped a close shave.

She shivered, her stomach lurching as the helicopter's engines whined, and it began to descend.

As they landed, Ella felt her pulse race. This wasn't how she had imagined their return, instead of being aided in the hunt, they were now suspects in the murder of two police officers.

She looked over to Brenner, who gave her hand a squeeze before they were led out of the helicopter and into a sea of cops. And that's where it became something of a blur, as Ella felt overloaded. Questions were thrown at them from every angle, and she could feel the weight of their eyes on her.

They were whisked away in waiting vehicles, taken rapidly out of the airfield.

Arriving at the precinct involved no less fanfare.

They were led to separate rooms, and Ella sat down in a metal chair, her hands cuffed behind her back. The room was sparse, with only a table and some chairs.

Her mind was racing as she tried to piece everything together. Brenner had told the truth, but without any proof, they were just two people accused of a heinous crime.

Suddenly the door opened, and a man walked in, dressed in a smart suit with slicked-back hair.

"Good evening, Miss Porter. I'm Detective Michaels. I've been assigned to your case," he said, sitting down across from her.

Ella eyed him warily. She knew better than to volunteer anything upfront at first. An interrogation was a dance.

"We have something of a dilemma on our hands, don't we?"

"The real killer is still out there," she said at last, deciding that someone had to speak first to move this along.

"Yes... well, I have some questions."

"So, what do you want to know?"

"I want to know everything," he replied, leaning forward. "I want you to tell me your version of events."

Ella took a deep breath, trying to gather her thoughts. "Haver was scared. He fled when we approached him. I found a bracelet on his desk tying him to our first victim."

"So you thought Haver was the killer?"

"Yes."

"So how'd he end up dead?"

"He was shot by the actual killer."

"Oh? And who was that?"

"I didn't see him."

"But you know it was a him? Not Marshall Gunn was it?"

"No," she said sharply.

He leaned back, crossing his arms over his neat suit. "You wouldn't have any reason to cover for Mr. Gunn, would you?"

There was an edge to his voice.

She decided not to reply.

"I was told... when you two were found... you were discovered in something of a compromising position."

She again didn't reply but could feel her face warming.

He studied her a moment, clearly intending to unnerve her, to make her uncomfortable. Hoping to force her to slip up. How often had she been on the other side of this table?

"Do you mind me asking why you two were naked, Ms. Porter?"

He didn't blink as he said it. Didn't urge the words forth as if displaying something gaudy, rather, he spoke them clinically, matter-of-factly.

She found her face was only reddening further. "I do mind," she said quietly. "But if you must know, I'd fallen in the river. I had to get warm."

"Quite. And he was naked because he'd also fallen in, hmm?"

She didn't like how he kept saying the word *naked*. But again, she kept her emotions in check. "He was checking on me," she said coolly. "He didn't want me to get hypothermia."

He nodded, still studying her. "And you were in the middle of this wilderness, investigating a murder, is that right?"

"That's correct."

He leaned forward again. "So, do you have any leads?"

She shook her head. "Not yet. We were closing in on Haver, but whoever it was that killed him and the other officer, they're still out there."

"Right," he said, tapping his pen against the table. "Well, it seems we have some work to do, then."

Ella bristled. They were wasting valuable time here, questioning her and Brenner. They should be out there, hunting the real killer.

"Can I ask you something?" she said, meeting his gaze.

"Of course."

"Why do you think we did it?"

He raised an eyebrow. "Why do I think you did it?"

She nodded. "Yes."

"Well," he said, taking a deep breath. "It's not every day that two suspects flee the scene of a double homicide, only to be found naked in the middle of nowhere. It doesn't look good, you have to admit."

"So you think we killed those officers?"

"I think it's a possibility," he said evenly. "But I also think there's more to the story. That's why we're here, asking questions."

Ella stared at him, her hands still cuffed behind her back. This was a nightmare. They were being treated like criminals while the real killer was out there, free to strike again. She wished she could make him understand, make him see the urgency of finding the true perpetrator. Her eyes darted towards the door then back again.

But Michaels was not budging, his eyes searing into hers as if he could read her every thought.

"Can you tell me about your relationship with Mr. Brenner?" he asked abruptly.

Ella felt her face flush again, this time in anger. What did their relationship have to do with anything? But she knew better than to show her emotions.

"There's nothing to tell," she said coolly. "We're partners, that's all."

"Partners," he repeated as if testing the word. "And yet, you were found naked together in the middle of nowhere. That's quite a partnership."

Ella gritted her teeth. This was getting nowhere. Again, he kept repeating the word *naked,* as if by saying it, he might expose her even further. And in a way, she found she was uncomfortable. She shifted awkwardly in the chair.

"Look," she said, deciding to take charge of the conversation. Playing nice was getting nowhere, so she switched tact. "I don't know what you want from us. We didn't kill those officers. We were trying to catch the real killer. And now we're being held here, while he's out there, free to kill again. So if you want to catch him, you need to let us go and let us do our job. Haver fired his own gun. Neither of our weapons will match the ballistics."

She held his gaze, willing him to believe her.

For a moment, there was silence. Then, Michaels leaned back in his chair, his eyes still fixed on hers.

"Okay," he said slowly. "I'll tell you what. We'll check that theory. If your guns are a match... we'll have problems."

"They won't match," she said.

"Well, good. Because we're running the shells right now."

She nodded in satisfaction but then stiffened. Her heart skipped a beat.

"What is it?" he said innocently. "You look troubled. Not changing your story, I hope?"

"No," she replied firmly.

But inwardly, she was starting to panic.

Evidence had already been tampered with at the precinct. The bracelet, the soil...

"Where is it being processed?"

"Hmm?"

"Are you processing ballistics *here*?"

"Where else?"

She went quiet.

Not good. If the real killer was still here, still hiding in the precinct, he might easily be able to mess with the match. He could frame Brenner and Ella for murder, and there was nothing they could do about it.

Chapter 32

Ella's heart pounded in her chest as she sat in the cold, dimly lit interrogation room. The harsh metal of the handcuffs dug into her wrists, a constant reminder of her predicament. She knew she had to escape before she was framed for a murder she didn't commit. Time was running out, and every passing second only heightened her anxiety.

The walls were a drab gray, adorned only with a faded motivational poster that had long lost its purpose. Ella's eyes darted around, searching for any opportunity to free herself from the cuffs.

Her interrogator was glancing at his phone now, tracking some series of alerts.

She glanced at the one-way mirror on the wall. The air in the room felt heavy, suffocating, as if it were closing in on her. But Ella refused to let fear paralyze her.

She felt confident that if the ballistics were being run at the lab downstairs, then she and Brenner were in serious trouble.

She had to reach the lab.

She had to escape the interrogation room first, which meant she had to escape the detective's supervision.

A glimmer of hope flickered in her mind as she recalled her confiscated phone. If only she could create a diversion, make the interrogator leave the room for a few precious moments. Her mind raced, searching for a plausible lie that would demand immediate attention. Then, it struck her.

Ella leaned forward, her voice trembling with desperation as she spoke to the interrogator. "Wait, I just remembered something. There's evidence on my phone. I have photos that can prove my innocence." She watched the flicker of curiosity cross the interrogator's face.

"What sort of photographs?"

"Photos that prove *everything*!" she insisted. Then, realizing she needed to sweeten the deal, she added, "How often does a prime murder suspect offer you the chance to peruse their private phone?"

He hesitated. The detective wrinkled his nose, but then his eyes flickered. He seemed to see the sense in this. He gave her a final, long look, saying, "We'll see, won't we?" before he rose from his chair and exited the room, leaving her alone.

As soon as the door closed, Ella knew she had to act fast. Ignoring the pain that surged through her hand, she twisted her wrist with sheer willpower, trying to dislocate her thumb. Beads of sweat formed on her forehead as she fought against the resistance of the handcuffs.

Finally, with a sharp crack, her thumb popped out of place, causing her excruciating pain but granting her freedom.

Taking a moment to catch her breath, adrenaline racing through her, Ella felt black spots dancing across her vision from the pain. Her thumb bent off at an odd angle.

She pushed the pain to the back of her mind and silently moved toward the door. She turned the handle cautiously, praying that it wouldn't creak and give her away. The door swung open with a barely audible whisper, and she slipped into the dimly lit hallway, her senses on high alert. Her thumb still throbbed, and she reached down, gritting her teeth, and pressed at the base of the knuckle, slipping the finger back into place with a grisly *pop*.

She nearly blacked out from the jolt of agony.

But once she'd settled and the pain subsided to a dull ache, her vision cleared of dark spots.

She was in the hall outside the interrogation room.

The sound of footsteps echoed in the distance, and Ella flattened herself against the wall, her heart pounding in her ears. A pair of uniformed officers walked past the entrance at the far end, engrossed in their conversation, oblivious to the fugitive lurking in their midst. She released a silent sigh of relief and resumed her stealthy journey through the labyrinthine corridors. Off to one side, through a window, she spotted Brenner sitting stony-faced in a chair, across from thre e officers.

Apparently, the police knew about Brenner's military background.

But they weren't the only ones.

The killer had known about the SEALs. Had known Brenner would be on scene.

He'd been taunting them all along.

And he was here, somewhere, hiding in plain sight. And what if...

Another thought struck her...

There was no way to weed out the killer. Not yet.

Not unless...

What if he really *was* going to tamper with the evidence? If she caught him in the act, perhaps that would be enough.

Ella frowned, moving in the shadows, one footstep padding after the other.

The hallway seemed to stretch endlessly, each door a potential threat. Ella moved with purpose, her steps light and calculated. She glanced at the signs on the walls, searching for the elusive "Evidence Room" that held the key to her freedom.

Finally, she spotted the sign she had been waiting for. It pointed her down a narrow corridor—this was a different route than the last time they'd come, searching for the laptop with the grisly pictures.

She hurried down the steps, taking them two at a time. She didn't even glance up to see if a security camera was watching her. What would the point have been, anyway?

Time was of the essence. She had to *move.* As she approached the door to the evidence room, her heart raced with anticipation. She knew she had to be quick, precise, and undetected. She thought of the officer serving as a clerk who'd been on sentry before.

Would he still be there? She leaned against the frame, and the door swung open soundlessly, revealing rows of shelves filled with boxes, folders, and evidence bags. She couldn't afford to waste time searching. She needed to locate the lab, and the last time she'd been down here, she thought she'd spotted an adjacent room.

At least for now, the desk was unoccupied.

Where was the evidence clerk?

She shivered.

Wondering if something bad had happened.

Wondering now if the killer was down here with her.

She froze. Her eyes scanned the room until they landed on the doorway at the far end. A low glow was coming from under the door.

With her hand throbbing in pain, Ella moved swiftly, weaving her way through the maze of evidence. She reached the door.

She could hear a voice on the other side. Two voices. One speaking in a blubbering, desperate voice.

"P-please!" the voice was saying. "Please!"

A familiar voice.

She frowned, hesitant, still standing on this side of the door. Her mind was speeding desperately now. She glanced back towards the evidence table.

She hesitated.

Someone who had access to evidence, like the laptop. Someone who had access to case files and FBI portfolios. Someone who could slip away without being seen for hours at a time during a work day.

She stared.

The desk clerk.

The large, hefty man who'd helped them earlier.

Why was he missing?

Who else in the entire precinct could slip away, tamper with evidence, and hijack APBs without being seen?

A cold dread settled on her.

The moaning voice from inside the evidence room had gone quiet now.

The evidence clerk was the killer.

She didn't even remember his name.

She frowned, turned, and pressed her eye to the keyhole.

There, inside the evidence room, she spotted a woman in a white lab coat, laying on the ground. Her hands were bound, and blood poured from a wound over her head.

"Please," the woman was mewling, her cheek resting against the cold floor. "P-please!"

Ella tensed.

And then she heard movement behind her. Coming from one of the evidence locker aisles.

She whirled around.

A heavy metal bat was being swung at her head, a small, yellow evidence label fluttering as it came arching towards her skull.

Chapter 33

Ella ducked just in time, feeling the whoosh of air from the bat as it narrowly missed her. Adrenaline fueled her movements as she kicked out at the evidence locker behind her, sending it crashing into the assailant. The impact knocked them both to the ground.

Breathless, Ella scrambled to her feet, ready to face her attacker. She gasped in horror as she realized who it was.

The evidence clerk lay sprawled on the ground, bleeding from a gash on his forehead. Ella's stomach churned as she saw the bat lying beside him—evidence of his intent to kill her.

He was snarling as he pushed to his feet now, his hefty frame causing him pause. But he moved far more spryly than a man of his size should've been able to.

In fact, the way he carried his ample frame reminded her of the man in the hood, in the thick coat. The man fleeing through the woods.

This was their killer.

But now, she was trapped in a basement, alone with the man.

She faced him, breathing heavily, her thumb still aching from where she'd dislocated it then slipped it back into joint.

He was picking up the bat a second time, a snarl twisting his face.

"What's my name?" he said slowly, fury in his eyes.

She blinked, still breathing heavily.

He gripped the bat tightly.

"What's my name!" he bellowed, his voice nearly a screech. "You don't know, do you?" he demanded, pointing the bat at her. "Do *you*?"

She scowled back at him. "You killed them? All of them?"

He was smirking now. "You thought you two were so clever. Didn't think I knew the laptop was there? The sin of pride." He was nodding now.

She noted a strange tattoo she hadn't spotted before, just on his wrist. An odd symbol, with a pyramid and different colored lines.

The man was waving his hands about now, the bat like a conductor's wand. "You sheep don't understand what's coming. What's coming for all of you!"

She knew he was just raving. Knew that she shouldn't bite. But her mind flitted to thoughts of the Collective.

She shivered in horror.

He was still ranting, swinging his arm with that strange tattoo about like a windmill. "It's coming for all of you! You think you can just ignore me? Hmm?"

She stared at him, blinked...

Drool was dribbling down the side of his cheek.

"My mother told me about your kind," he whispered. "Sheep and goats. They're all sheep and goats. What are you? Vain? Lustful?"

"What are you?" she said.

"No-Name. You can call me No-Name, because no one knows my name. You don't do you, pretty lady? They never do. So what are you? Envious?"

"Bored," she said, suddenly. And she didn't even know where the words had conjured from. A strange, righteous indignation had arisen within her. "That's why? You killed them because they ignored you?"

"What?"

"You're just a petty, little man, aren't you?"

For a moment, she almost forgot the danger. All of this... the melodrama, the staged scenes. The traps on the road from the airport, the intercepted APBs... The photographs with the seven deadly sins. The murders spanning back years... Murders only one person could've kept hidden. A cop.

This cop.

This small, sad, little man trapped in a basement. Murderous out of neglect.

She found herself sneering, glaring at him.

This, it turned out, didn't calm him down.

"Wrath!" he screamed.

He raised his bat and charged at her.

Ella's heart pounded as her contempt was replaced by a sudden burst of healthy fear. But instead of facing him, she spun on her heel and sprinted into the evidence room, her pursuer hot on her heels. The dimly lit room was lined with rows of shelves, filled with an assortment of evidence from past cases. As her eyes darted furtively about, while on the move, surveying it like a blur of color, her eyes widened at the myriad of potential weapons and obstacles.

No-Name, a hulking figure with a cold and determined expression, closed in on Ella, his bat held tightly in his hands. His muscular frame loomed over her, giving him a clear advantage in terms of strength. Ella, however, refused to succumb to fear, her survival instinct kicking into high gear.

With a swift movement, No-Name swung the bat toward Ella's head. She barely managed to duck, feeling the wind of the weapon as it whizzed by her. In her panic, she grabbed the nearest item within reach, a heavy chain—rusted, stained, and tagged with a yellow badge—and hurled it at No-Name. The chain slammed into his chest, momentarily stunning him and buying Ella some time.

As Ella scrambled to her feet, she glanced at the shelves around her, searching for anything that could turn the tide in her favor. Her eyes fell upon a shelf of glass bottles containing various liquids and powders. With a calculated aim, she lunged forward, pushing the shelf with all her strength. The bottles crashed to the ground, shattering into a colorful and chaotic mess. The room filled with a thick cloud of smoke as the volatile substances mixed together, creating a temporary cover.

She wasn't sure, but it looked like the residue of some recently raided meth lab.

She tried not to breathe the fumes.

Through the haze, Ella stumbled across a stack of filing cabinets, knocking them over to create a makeshift barricade. The metal cabinets toppled with a resounding crash, forming an obstacle course between her and No-Name. As she made her way through the narrow gaps, she could hear No-Name's heavy footsteps drawing closer.

Her eyes kept moving along the shelves. Fire extinguisher, no... a stone—no, just foam. Files. Folders... Shit. Where was... There! That would work!

Desperation fueled her movements as she reached for a large box of confiscated knives. She tore open the box, the blades glinting menacingly in the dim light. With a newfound weapon in hand, she turned to face No-Name, determination etched on her face.

No-Name charged at Ella, swinging his bat with brute force. She dodged his blows with agile movements, the adrenaline coursing through her veins. Ella lunged forward, slashing at No-Name with one of the knives, leaving a shallow cut across his arm. No-Name howled in pain, momentarily disoriented and taken aback that the woman half his size had tried to fight back.

Taking advantage of the opening, Ella picked up a nearby evidence bag filled with ball bearings and hurled it at No-Name's feet. The bag exploded upon impact, scattering the metallic, oil-slick spheres across the floor. No-Name's footing faltered, and he slipped, crashing heavily onto the hard surface.

Ella didn't waste a second. She rushed toward the nearest shelf and grabbed hold of it, wrenching it away from the wall. As she dragged it toward No-Name, various items spilled from the shelves, adding to the chaos of the room. Old, obsolete guns tumbled off the walls, photographs fluttered through the air, and fragile pieces of evidence shattered on impact.

With her last ounce of strength, Ella pushed the shelf down onto No-Name, the weight of it pinning him to the ground. He struggled against the confinement, his attempts to break free futile.

Gasping for breath, Ella crawled through the narrow gap between the shelves, emerging on the other side. She pushed the shelf further, wedging it tightly against the wall, effectively trapping No-Name beneath its weight. The room fell silent, the only sound echoing through the air being No-Name's frustrated growls.

Ella staggered to her feet, her body bruised and battered.

"They'll never believe you!" No-Name was grunting, his voice strained. "Come back here!"

Ella turned, facing the room with the bound lab assistant. "They don't have to believe me," she muttered. "They just have to believe *her*."

She strode hurriedly towards the woman tied on the floor, a swell of relief flooding through her.

Epilogue

Ella and Brenner sat huddled together on a small plane cutting over the deep ocean as they were flown back to Nome.

Home sweet home.

Where daddy dearest waited.

Where her sister waited. Where so many bad memories lingered.

She glanced at her phone again, double-checking the update. The lab assistant was going to make a full recovery, and the woman had corroborated Ella's story in full.

No-Name was the killer. They'd found evidence proving it buried in his backyard—the location had been discovered by Brenner's perceptive eye. And the rich, fertile soil on the man's boots.

"No SEAL would've made that mistake," Brenner had said at the start of their flight.

Now, the handsome man was dozing, his head leaning against her.

She didn't move. She liked the feeling of his warmth.

She smiled faintly, reaching up and combing his hair.

The pilot adjusted his green headset, peering through the night, watching the glow from the small, gold-mining town far below.

They weren't descending yet, and for a moment, Ella almost wished they could stay there, suspended in the sky... forever, maybe.

Her and Brenner.

She smiled.

She watched the way the glow from the moon caught Brenner's features. And then, through the window, a flash of green.

She blinked. Blues and purples.

Her eyes widened.

The Northern Lights, dancing, dancing, dancing. Creating a spectacle just for the two of them.

For a moment, she considered waking Brenner, but he'd been in Nome far longer than her. No... he needed his rest.

Her thumb still ached as she left it on her lap, near her phone. Her other hand kept stroking Brenner's hair, softly.

His eyelashes really were quite long. She wondered just how prickly his five-o-clock shadow would feel against her lips.

A small smile caused her lips to begin to curl.

And then her phone buzzed.

Once.

Twice.

Then nothing.

She frowned, glancing down.

And then she froze.

It was as if all the warmth bled out of her.

She stared, stunned at the message from an unknown number.

Here in your motel. Come see me. We need to talk.

She re-read the message and then swallowed.

She didn't need a number to know who this was.

Mortimer Graves was back in town.

She'd thought he'd dodged her call when she'd asked him about the Collective.

But instead...

He'd flown into Nome just to see her.

She felt another little shiver, staring at the glowing screen of her phone. The Northern Lights danced outside her window in streaks across the sky. A handsome man reclined against her shoulder.

But none of it could soothe the cold knot now forming in her stomach.

The Graveyard Killer was back in town.

Bringing up the Collective had served as something of a summoning.

But why?

What on earth was going on?

The plane jolted, hitting some turbulence, and a couple of lights flickered. And then the pilot pushed the controls, and the plane began to veer in a circling descent.

Ella couldn't shake the feeling that they now looked like some bird of prey, circling a dying corpse.

What's Next for Ella Porter?

Girl Who Freezes Shadows

The Mendenhall glacier holds more than just ancient secrets—it conceals a serial killer's gruesome handiwork. As bodies begin to surface, perfectly preserved by the ice and hauntingly displayed through the art of taxidermy, an intense game of cat and mouse ensues, pushing FBI agent Ella Porter to her limits.

Ella Porter, a tenacious and brilliant agent with an instinct for unravelling the darkest of mysteries, must navigate the treacherous Alaskan wilderness to stop this sadistic murderer.

But when two men are sent to find her, Ella turns from hunter to hunted, and soon discovers that everyone she loves could be in danger.

With each victim unearthed, the intricate taxidermy artistry raises haunting questions about the killer's motives and his twisted fascination with preserving life in death.

A pulse-pounding, atmospheric thriller that will keep you on the edge of your seat until the very last page. Prepare to immerse yourself in the depths of an Alaskan winter, where the bone-chilling suspense will freeze your blood and the race against a cunning murderer will leave you breathless. Can Ella Porter uncover the truth and stop the killer before she becomes the next victim? Find out in this gripping tale of terror, survival, and the pursuit of justice in the most unforgiving of landscapes.

Other Books by Georgia Wagner

A picture containing text, sign

Description automatically generated

The skeletons in her closet are twitching... Genius chess master and FBI consultant Artemis Blythe swore she'd never return to the misty Cascade Mountains.Her father—a notorious serial killer, responsible for the deaths of seven women—is now imprisoned, in no small part due to a clue she provided nearly fifteen years ago.And now her father wants his vengeance.A new serial killer is hunting the wealthy and the elite in the town of Pinelake. Artemis' father claims he knows the identity of the killer, but he'll only tell daughter dearest. Against her will, she finds herself forced back to her old stomping grounds.Once known as a child chess prodigy, now the locals only think of her as 'The Ghostkiller's' daughter.In the face of a shamed family name and a brother involved with the Seattle mob, Artemis endeavors to use her tactical genius to solve the baffling case.Hunting a murderer who strikes without a trace, if she fails, the next skeleton in her closet will be her own.

Other Books by Georgia Wagner

A cold knife, a brutal laugh. Then the odds-defying escape.

Once a hypnotist with her own TV show, now, Sophie Quinn works as a full-time consultant for the FBI. Everything changed six years ago. She can still remember that horrible night. Slated to be the River Killer's tenth victim, she managed to slip her bindings and barely escape where so many others failed. Her sister wasn't so lucky.

And now the killer is back.

Two PHDs later, she's now a rising star at the FBI. Her photographic memory helps solve crimes, but also helps her to never forget. She saw the River Killer's tattoo. She knows what he sounds like. And now, ten years later, he's active again.

Sophie Quinn heads back home to the swamps of Louisiana, along the Mississippi River, intent on evening the score and finding the man who killed her sister. It's been six years since she's been home, though. Broken relationships and shattered dreams exist among the bayous, the rivers, the waterways and swamps of Louisiana; can Sophie find her way home again? Or will she be the River Killer's next victim to float downstream?

Want to know more?

Greenfield press is the brainchild of bestselling author Steve Higgs. He specializes in writing fast paced adventurous mystery and urban fantasy with a humorous lilt. Having made his money publishing his own work, Steve went looking for a few 'special' authors whose work he believed in.

Georgia Wagner was the first of those, but to find out more and to be the first to hear about new releases and what is coming next, you can join the Facebook group by copying the following link into your browser - www.facebook.com/GreenfieldPress

About the Author

Georgia Wagner worked as a ghost writer for many, many years before finally taking the plunge into self-publishing. Location and character are two big factors for Georgia, and getting those right allows the story to flow seamlessly onto the page. And flow it does, because Georgia is so prolific a new term is required to describe the rate at which nerve-tingling stories find their way into print.

When not found attached to a laptop, Georgia likes spending time in local arboretums, among the trees and ponds. An avid cultivator of orchids, begonias, and all things floral, Georgia also has a strong penchant for art, paintings, and sculptures. A many-decades long passion for mystery novels.

Printed in Great Britain
by Amazon